THE STONE GARDEN

G·K
Hall
&Cᵒ

Also by Bill Brooks
in Large Print:

Buscadero

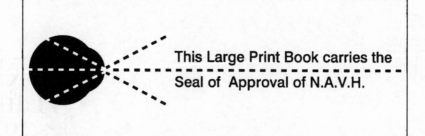

This Large Print Book carries the
Seal of Approval of N.A.V.H.

THE STONE GARDEN

GARDEN

The Epic Life of Billy the Kid

BILL BROOKS

Thorndike Press • Waterville, Maine

Published in 2001 by arrangement with
Tom Doherty Associates, LLC.

G.K. Hall Large Print Western Series.

The text of this Large Print edition is unabridged.
Other aspects of the book may vary from the original edition.

Set in 16 pt. Plantin.

Printed in the United States on permanent paper.

Library of Congress Cataloging-in-Publication Data

Brooks, Bill, 1943–
     The stone garden : the epic life of Billy the Kid / Bill Brooks.
       p. cm
     ISBN 0-7838-9639-5 (lg. print : hc : alk. paper)
     1. Billy the Kid — Fiction. 2. Outlaws — Fiction. 3. Large type
books. I. Title.
PS3552.R65863 S76 2001b
   813′.54—dc21   2001053247

*For my wife, Diane, whose love and support
continues to carry me across the
desert of time and doubt*

BOOK ONE

BOOK ONE

1

WE OWE RESPECT TO THE LIVING; TO THE DEAD, WE OWE ONLY TRUTH.

— VOLTAIRE

Garrett claimed he shot me through the heart, through the head, through the mouth. I'm not dead. Nobody believed him, not even his own deputy, Poe, who was standing outside Pete Maxwell's house smoking a shuck.

"Pat, I believe you have killed the wrong man." His words, not mine.

But it was too late to admit it on his part, so he lied. "No, I'm sure it was the Kid. I could tell from his voice."

Tell me how one man knows another in a pitch-black room? How one man shoots another through the heart in the blackness? I can understand Garrett to lie like that. Poe and McKinney I can understand too — they never even met me. Me and Garrett done things he would be ashamed to tell of. He lied because of the fat reward the territory had on me. He lied because he was scared. He lied about a lot of things. I don't forget. I don't forget.

But shoot me? Kill me? My luck's not so bad or his so good that he could have ever shot me through the heart or head, or even the ankle bone, that night or any other. For one thing, I was a hundred miles away with a married woman I won't name now.

Who Garrett killed that night with one damn lucky shot was Billy Barlow, a handsome boy like me, about my size and color, and it would have been easy to identify him had Garrett not made a habit of notching crosses in the heads of his bullets so that when they struck muscle and bone they flattened out and tore up everything in their path — a trick he learned as a buffalo killer. And what Garrett's notched bullet struck that night there in that pitch-dark room was the back of poor Billy Barlow's head, blowing away half his face coming out and splashing his brains all over Pedro's walls. So it was easy for Garrett to say it was me he'd killed and not the "wrong man." But Poe had it right.

They say Celsa went crazy with grief and cussed Garrett like he was a rabid dog. "Usted es un cobarde ninguno hijo bueno de una perra!" Calling him a no-good cowardly son of a bitch right to his face.

I found all this out much later from some folks I knew in Fort Sumner who knew the truth and would not lie to me but were afraid of Garrett and the climate in Lincoln County at the time. They said Billy Barlow's eyes were gone and

10

most of his forehead. They said his face was like a watermelon struck by a sledge, just blood and bone and gristle. Even his dear mother would not have known him.

Pete was afraid to sleep in the room after that and never did. They say that until it got washed away in the flood, Billy Barlow's ghost could be seen looking from the windows of Pete's house, that candles lit themselves, and Pete could hear Billy's boots clomping around after everybody went to bed. It turned Pete's hair white and led to his early death.

If it had not been that I'd found my fortune elsewhere, I would have looked Garrett up in front of all his friends and said, "I guess you killed the wrong goddamn man, Pat," and given him a chance to do it right this time — him looking me in the eyes — and see what he could have done with me.

But I let it go for reasons I'll explain when I get around to that part.

They wrapped Billy Barlow in a horse blanket, trussed it with baling wire, and dropped his body in a hole and had six men (the same number that carries a coffin) sign a coroner's report stating it was me: Dead, dead, dead.

We the jury unanimously find that William Bonney was killed by a shot in the left breast, in the region of the heart, fired from a pistol in the hand of Patrick F. Garrett, and our verdict is that the act of the said Garrett was jus-

11

tifiable homicide, and we are unanimous in the opinion that the gratitude of the whole community is due the said Garrett for his act and that he deserves to be rewarded.

M. Rudulph, President
Anton Sabedra
Pedro Anto Lucero
Jose X Silba
Sabal X Gutierrez
Lorenzo X Jaramillo

Homicide is correct, but not of me, of Billy Barlow. I'll tell you something else too. Ol' Sabal Gutierrez was jealous of me because of his wife, Celsa, and the fact she liked dancing with me and we'd sometimes go for long walks along the river and he didn't like it but was scared to death to do anything about it. I guess he thought there was more to it (and in truth, there was) and I guess he was glad to Jesus to be rid of me and happy enough to sign whatever Garrett put in front of him. But hoping a man's dead don't make it so, not in Garrett's eyes or Sabal's.

I'll tell you something else I found out too. Half those men on that list weren't even there and ol' Sabal, with his pitted face and merciless eyes, was himself Garrett's brother-in-law. If Garrett told him to say he'd screwed the Virgin Mary, he would. How would any of them know who was in that lonesome grave, late at night as it was and half of Billy's face shot away?

Garrett took his chances, figuring I wouldn't

12

come back and show him up for the liar he was once he had me killed because every law in the territory was also looking for me. Looking to hang me again. He had nothing to lose. He'd get his blood money and whatever political office he had in mind, and if I did show my face he'd shoot it off again, or try. The queer thing is, he'd talked about it several times before, on moonlit nights with tequila setting fires in our brains.

"Look at us," he'd say. "Getting nowhere fast." His long legs stretched out while senoritas danced around him, sat on his lap, nibbled his ears.

"We are simply hostages of our times, Pat," I would say, and he would blink and act surprised I would say such things, when in truth he knew I was fairly good with words, writing them or talking them. Tunstall gave me books to read and got me interested in the power of words.

"Nam et ipsa scientia ptestas est," Tunstall said on a frightful night when lightning danced up and down the Pecos Valley.

"What's that mean, John?" I asked him.

"That's Latin, Henry. It means: 'Knowledge itself is power.' "

I never forgot that. Sometimes I'd say things like that to Pat when we were skunk drunk and whoring.

"Cuss you, Kid, for such high talk," he'd say, his eyes aglaze with liquor and dreamy thoughts.

"My favorite thing besides drinking with you, Pat, and stealing cattle and dancing with pretty

13

girls, is reading books. A fella can learn a lot from just reading books."

"Someday I might write a book on you, Kid," he said this one particular time when we were whiling away our time in Mesilla. We were sitting around Francisco's cantina across the square from the Catholic church and had just finished eating beefsteaks fried with chilies and smothered with frijoles that we washed down with ice beer. Later we got drunk as sin and paid some senoritas to wash our hair and take baths with us. We played like happy children without a care in the world. We'd trade the girls off, laughing and dropping the soap and trying to find it again until we exhausted ourselves and they were practically asleep from all the activity me and Pat gave them. Then we took up drinking again in the cantina and got back on the subject.

"What sort of book would you write, Pat?" I said. I had to laugh, he was so goddamn funny, sitting there long tall Sally, his face crooked with liquor. When he was drunk like that he talked out of the side of his mouth like everything was a secret.

"How I killed you, Kid," he said.

"You better be careful, Pat. You know that kind of talk don't hold water with me."

I thought he'd laugh, but he didn't. I didn't either. Talk like that, you can't be too careful. I was right to be cautious considering what later happened in Sumner.

"I could claim I killed you," he said, "make a big show of it, and you could lay low, take on a new name, go to Texas, California maybe, make something of yourself. You're young yet."

"Why would I want to do that when I'm having as much fun as a man can have right here in Lincoln County?" I said.

"I was just thinking, is all," he said. Then the senorita bit him on the lip and drew blood and he didn't know whether to slap her or push up her skirts.

We slept that night in the same bed, back to back, and I listened to him snore and wondered if I shouldn't place my pistol in his ear and blow out his brains just to make sure he didn't do it to me first. I knew that night, after his talk of running me out of the country, things had changed between us. Nothing would ever be the same.

The next morning, as we got ready to ride back to ol' Fort Sumner, I said, "You know, Pat, I was thinking. Maybe I'll write a book on you someday."

He just looked at me over the back of his horse as he was tightening up the cinch strap and right then I knew we'd reached the end of our string.

I'm not surprised he finally "killed" me. In a way it showed enterprise. Pat was always an enterprising sort. He rode a long time on my coattails after writing that book on me, and even got President Roosevelt to appoint him customs inspector of El Paso before someone caught him out in the desert and shot him in the back while

15

he was pissing on a cactus. Some claim it was a bald-headed cowboy named Wayne Brazil — but Brazil got acquitted and for good reason. They say Wayne laughed and laughed every time someone asked him about it. It went as an unsolved murder.

Poor Pat, didn't he know that what goes around comes around?

Didn't he know that if you bargain with the devil, you'll end up in his bed?

Didn't he know that I never forget a friend, or an enemy?

I don't forget.

2

WHO CAN CONTROL HIS FATE?
— SHAKESPEARE

Bonita, near Camp Grant, A.T.

"*Hey,* kid!"

It was that damn smithy bellering like he was gassed up. Cahill, I believe they said his name was; a real piss pot, mean drunk and looking for something easy I guess, and that was me in his eyes, who didn't weigh so much as one of his legs.

I was down on my luck and only in camp a week. Pockets empty, looking for work. Horse and saddle, pistol and rifle, the clothes I had on my back. A box of cartridges and an extra pair of socks in my saddlebags, and two books. That's all I owned to my name. Not much work but plenty of hell to be raised in that territory and I was doing my best to raise all I could. Rather dance than work any day. Always did, always will.

This Cahill, or Cayhall, hammered horseshoes

17

over on the post. You could hear the ring of his hammer all day long — ring, ring, ring. And when the wind was right, you could smell the soot of his forge, see the sparks fly, hear the nicker of horses as he nailed the shoes to their feet.

But come dark, he quit hammering and started drinking in the whiskey tents. The only drinking establishments for fifty miles in any direction unless you wanted to drink Apache beer and suffer the shits. They had one tent set up for officers and one for the enlisted men and civilians. A man named Poteet owned them both. He had an Apache wife and seven or eight children and slept with a shotgun under his bed. Rumor had it he was wanted for several killings in Missouri.

I'd heard some ugly talk about this Cahill, or Cayhall, how he dallied with some of the young soldiers, offering them money to creep off into the shadows with him. Some did, they say. I was sipping on a ten-cent beer and staring at my image in the glass when I heard his bluster. I half-turned around and he slapped me between the shoulders. It stung and the fire rose in my neck and burned my ears.

"You're a little toot," he said, looking down at me, grinning like a fox that had just caught himself a chicken.

I was quick to anger in those days — still am over certain things. Manuella says I've got too much temper still, threatens to leave me all the time, but she never will, temper or no temper.

"Leave off, mister." That slap had got me red-hot in more ways than one.

He leaned in close and I could see the wormy red veins in his nose and smell his greasy breath and see the way his eyes tried to swallow me up.

"Hey'a, let me buy you a drink there, darling," he said, then slapped his big mitt on the plank bar and ordered up two whiskeys. Mule Ear, I think it said on the label. He pushed one my way, then waited for me to pick it up and drink and thank him for the privilege, I suppose. But I knew that would be my mistake if I did. I played it off, his offer, and when he saw I wasn't going to drink with him he laid one hand on my shoulder and squeezed.

"I seen you around," he said. "Been keeping my eye on you." Like that meant something to me. I figured it was just as well to clear out as to get into a row with a man two or three times my size, and him armed with a belly gun. I could see the butt of his pistol protruding from his belt, his big gut pressing down on it. I tried tugging my shoulder from his grip but he held on and wouldn't let go.

"What do you want with me?" I said loud as you please for all to hear; I wanted to show him up for what he was: a low son of a bitch who would force himself on a boy who wasn't doing anything but minding his own business.

It got quiet around us then, him still holding on to me. Some soldiers and buffalo skinners held fast, waiting to see what was going to happen next. Entertainment was scarce in that place.

"I'll slap you down like a puta!" he said, and this time his free hand came around and clipped me two or three times hard against the mouth and split my lips and caused me to see stars.

I grabbed hold of his wrists with both my hands to keep him from slapping me more but he was strong and shoved me to the floor, then climbed atop me trying to pin my arms with his knees. It was like having a wagon roll on me, all that weight.

He slapped me two or three times more and I couldn't figure why one of those soldiers didn't try and stop him except they were all a bunch of yellow cowards. The Indians they'd come to fight didn't have much to worry about with that bunch if they wouldn't pull a full grown man off a fifteen-year-old boy.

Something strange happened in my head. The more he slapped me, the more angry I became, and all that anger just built and built until I got a hand free just as he was unbuttoning the front of his trousers.

"I'm gonna give you something to think about, you little puta," he cawed, fumbling with himself while trying to hold me down. Still nobody stepped in and said, "Git off that boy, Cahill. It ain't right what you are doing." Nobody.

He about had it out of his pants when I got my hand free and jerked that pistol from his belt and punched the barrel into his gut and pulled the trigger.

The gunshot was loud, shattering the held-breath silence. His body jerked upright. It was like somebody stuck a pig, the way the blood shot out of him. His hot blood spilled over my hands, the gun, down my wrists, soaking the cuffs of my shirt wetly red like wine spilled on them. I saw his face through the haze of blue smoke from the revolver. It was twisted, his teeth were biting down on his tongue.

He went *"Ooof"* and toppled over, still holding himself like someone had brained him from behind. The shot set fire to his shirt and someone took a bucket of beer and doused the flames. He gasped like a fish. I guess all his tough talk had found another mouth to live in.

He was still dying when I left Bonita that night under a sky full of stars and the moon, riding the Santa Ritas.

Tom Cahill, or Cayhall, was the first man I ever killed.

3

OF COMFORT NO MAN SPEAK:
LET'S TALK OF GRAVES, OF WORMS,
   AND EPITAPHS;
MAKE DUST OUR PAPER, AND WITH
   RAINY EYES
WRITE SORROW ON THE BOSOM OF
   THE EARTH.

                — SHAKESPEARE

Garrett buried me between Tom and Charlie in the old military graveyard. Across from us sleeps:

> *Roberto Salazar.*
> *Juanita Delgado* and her infant child unnamed.
> *Garza.* An angel carved in the headstone above his name.
> *Unknown.* A pair of praying hands. A rose. Songbirds.

Charlie's all bones, Tom is too. I sleep peaceful between them.

The seasons change, the dead sleep on.

Mex, gringo, man woman child. We're all the same.

Rich man, poor man. White or brown. We're all the same.

Garrett rides by on a snow-white horse. Sold his soul for a badge and a promise, but he'll never see that five hundred dollars reward money Wallace put on my head because even Wallace doesn't believe he killed the Kid.

Celsa came and put flowers on our grave. She thought Garrett told the truth, cursed him like a dog for what he did. Blood everywhere. How could she have known it wasn't me? Sabal beat her constantly for her flagrant desire, but still she came, sick with passion. Love is a fever that burns hot in the blood and can't be cured.

I stayed in some sheep camps after and asked the old men if they'd heard that Billy the Kid was killed by Garrett in Fort Sumner. They shook their heads and all said the same thing:

"We don't believe it."

The music plays — guitars and brass horns — and in the plaza the young girls dance, their eyes bright, searching the faces of the young men to see if *Billy* is among them. And sometimes he is, while Garrett rides a white horse, his own mind doubtful, his hands folded atop the pommel as if in prayer. His soul is a pinata twisting in the wind, being struck blows by laughing children whose mothers despair that he has sent their

Billy to his grave.

Above our heads, the Mexican carver, Ramon Salas, chiseled our names into a block of stone that within a year was chipped away, the stone chips given as charms to the self-same children, the old men saying, "From the grave of El Chivato and his companeros."

Garrett rides a ghost-white horse, his belly full of lies and dust.

Celsa weeps under the scornful bitter eye of her husband.

Wallace sleeps on a feather bed in Santa Fe across from the plaza where the young girls dance.

Life is a circle that has no beginning, no end.

Tom, Charlie, and me sleep like babes in innocent death, while Garrett dips our bones in blood and writes our history.

4

**MY THOUGHTLESS YOUTH WAS WINGED
WITH VAIN DESIRES,
MY MANHOOD, LONG MISLED BY
WANDERING FIRES.**

— DRYDEN

Me and Tom stretched out on the banks of the Canadian, looking up at the clouds passing overhead and making things out of them.

"That one looks like a pirate's head," Tom said. I couldn't see how.

"A girl riding a horse," I said about one. He laughed.

Sun glittered in the water like a thousand candle flames and wind rustled the leaves on the cottonwoods and ruffled Tom's hair. It was thick and red and had a cowlick he couldn't keep combed down.

"I think someday I will go east and see what all the talk is about," he said.

"I've been there and it's really something," I told him.

He didn't believe me because he thought I was

fooling around again.

"I bet you ain't been farther east than Amarillo," he said.

"New York," I said. "I was born there."

"I thought you said Silver City?"

"No, that's where my mother passed on." I could see her clear gray eyes still, the stare of death in them. I thought of Joe and where he went and what he was doing while me and Tom were lying on our backs making things up out of the clouds. We were never close, not like brothers should be. Him gone, me gone. He could be dead. I could be too, in his eyes.

"Is it true you robbed a Chinaman of his laundry," Tom said, "and the sheriff locked you up in his jail and you made your escape out the chimney?"

I laughed.

"I was a mean rascal, Tom. Everybody knew it and that Chinaman lied like sin. Why would I want to steal somebody's dirty wet drawers?"

He laughed.

"How many girls you had?" he said.

His face blotched red.

"Plenty," I said, but in truth I hadn't had a single one yet, though I'd spent a lot of time thinking about it.

"I bet we could ride into town and find us a girl and you wouldn't know what to do with her," he cawed. Truth be told, I did want to go find out what having a girl was like. I'd already killed a man and tasted liquor and learned to smoke. I figured it was about time I learned the rest of what there was to becoming a man, and Tom needed to learn too if we were going to ride together and be pals, so I took him up on his bet.

"Shoot," I said, "let's go."

So we went. Rode straight into Ciudad Juarez where we heard there was a cathouse called the Red Lady and if you had the money you could get just about anything in the way of sexual pleasure you wanted. We had saved up our earnings from some stolen beeves we'd run between the Panhandle and Fort Sumner and were flush and ready to get started on our way to becoming real men. We rode with our thoughts of having our first woman popping in our brains like fat grasshoppers on a hot day.

When we got to town the sheriff, a short, brown Mexican, was overseeing a cockfight in the middle of the main drag. He had a hatful of dollars from taking up bets and was yelling at a man wearing an eye patch and holding a big blood-red rooster. The rooster's feathers were sleek in the noonday sun — it had little yellow fierce eyes and razor-sharp metal spurs on its feet.

"Arriba," cried the sheriff, waving his hatful of money.

Then the man wearing the eye patch flung the rooster into the ring the men had formed and the two birds — the rooster and a white cock — took after each other, their wings beating the air, their squawks like rusty door hinges, as they locked up, pecking and spurring each other. In less than a minute the white cock lay dead, a heap of bloody feathers. The red rooster was pecking at its eyes.

Me and Tom didn't wait to see the next fight.

We asked a vaquero where we might find the cathouse and he said we should go right up the street and turn down the alley. We thanked him for the information and rode the way he told us.

"You still want to do it?" Tom said, his cowlick sticking up like rooster feathers when he took his hat off and wiped the sweat from his face.

"I didn't ride all this way just to watch chickens fight," I said, acting brave, like I'd been with plenty of girls before and it wasn't anything to me to get excited over. "You?"

"Nah, but you first then," Tom said as we reined in our horses at probably the only structure in town that wasn't adobe. It had a long low roof over a gallery where men sat in chairs and stood leaning against the roof poles. Some were smoking and some spitting and some talking to one another like they were waiting for a train. They all took notice of me and Tom as we rode up. I guess that was their job, to watch everything, the way it looked like.

"This the Red Lady?" I asked one of the men. He looked like a banker and wore a gray suit and a gray hat and even his beard was gray. I could tell he was from north of the border.

He talked around his cigar.

"You boys ain't got wet yet, have you?"

"What's that supposed to mean?" Tom said.

"Hell, son, it means what it means." He spat between his boots. Some of the others grinned, and I could feel the anger heating up in my blood. But I didn't come here to fight no more than I'd come to watch chickens fight. I got off my horse, walked past those boys, and knocked on the door and waited.

Nobody answered right away and I looked round at Tom and he looked at me.

"Maybe they're all busy," he said. "Maybe we oughter come back later."

I was about ready to agree with him. It wasn't just I was a little nervous about what we were getting into, it was also those men grinning at us like we were fools. I knocked again. The door opened. The woman standing there was about as old as my mother, tall, still some good-looking. I guess she was a breed, half-white, half-Mex, by the fair color of her skin, the blue eyes. She wore a blue silk kimono, loose, so I could see some of what I might be buying.

"Well, what we got here," she said. "You little yahoos lost?"

I looked at Tom. He was tugging his hat low over his eyes.

"Do we look like we're lost?" I said.

"Oh, I just thought you boys might be looking for the mercantile, to buy some rock candy."

"I guess you don't want our business," I said. "We could find us another cathouse that does."

29

"You're a feisty little thing, ain't you?"

"I guess I am." I chucked my head for Tom to get down off his horse and follow us inside.

I scraped my boots and Tom scraped his and we took our hats off and held them in our hands as the woman led us into a parlor where several gals sat around. One of them was reading the Police Gazette. Most just had on kimonos, stockings, but showing a lot of their wares. One was buck-toothed when she smiled, and another had a lazy eye. One was fat and another skinny. One had her hair cut short as a boy's.

"How much?" I asked the woman who had greeted me at the door.

"Depends on which one you pick," she said.

I looked at Tom.

"You pick you one," I said.

He looked them over, picked the skinny one with the short hair.

"How about her?"

"That's Rose," the woman said. "She's three dollars."

"Go on," I said to Tom, nudging him in the ribs as I reached in my pocket for our fun money. Soon as I paid the woman, the skinny gal came and took Tom by the hand and led him off down a hallway where there were several doors painted different colors.

"What about you, Feisty?" the woman said. I looked them all over.

"I guess I didn't ride this far to do my dealing

30

with the hired help," I said. "How high a price you get?"

She raised a hand to the top of her kimono like she was a little surprised.

"Darling, you sure you want to spend that kind of money?"

"I reckon it ain't every day I get down this way. Might as well go full bore."

"I hope you're a real broncobuster," she said, putting her arm around me.

We went down the hall, all the way to the back room where there was a big brass bed in the center and wine-colored drapes over the windows and a cart filled with liquor bottles. The room smelled like hollyhocks.

"You didn't ask me how much I was," she said, slipping out of her kimono.

"I ain't concerned," I said.

"It'll cost you ten dollars, darling, if you want this to go any further."

I took out twenty, tossed it on the bed.

"Well, I guess you're a broncobuster extraordinaire," she said. "Why not get out of them duds and let's get to riding."

I guess we were finishing up with the first course when she asked me my name.

"Billy," I said. "But my mama named me Henry."

"I like Henry better," she said. "Mine's Belle."

"Henry and Belle," I said. "Sounds like leaders of an outlaw gang."

"Don't it though."

Her mouth tasted like wet peaches and I sure always had a hunger for wet peaches. At one point while I was trying to get her full broke, she said, "Why is it all the little fellas have big ones, do you think?"

I felt like that fighting rooster.

Several times she called out my name, "Oh, Billy, oh, Henry!" like that, and I thought maybe I was hurting her some, but she just laughed when I asked her and said, "Just keep right on a-hurting me, darling."

Every once in a while we'd take a break and swallow some of that fine liquor she had and smoke a cigar, then get back to it. I finally said, "I reckon I about used up all that twenty dollars, ain't I?"

"I reckon so, but we're off the clock now, don't worry about it."

And so I didn't.

Later on when Tom and me were setting up camp back on the Canadian, he looked at me and said, "You know what that gal Rose told me?"

"No," I said.

"That she'd never been with a man big as me and asked if I'd go gentle with her. Gawd almighty, I liked to have died when she said that."

I rolled up in my blankets that night thinking how easy it is for a man to be fooled by sweet words. How easy it is to get to thinking you're something you're not. I thought of Cahill back in that whiskey tent thinking he was tough and mean, a man who could have his way whenever he wanted it when all he really was, was a dirty son of a bitch who got one in the guts and died as easy as a sparrow.

And I thought about me and Tom and how easy Rose and Belle made us feel like big roosters when all we were most likely were sparrows waiting to get shot off a telegraph wire by a woman's pretty words, and how any man could be a sparrow if he had a few dollars in his pockets and a big loneliness in his heart.

But knowing such truths didn't keep us from going back the next day. And we kept returning until we were broke, falling more and more in love with Rose and Belle each time we went. Every now and then I think about Belle and wonder whatever happened to her, wonder if she is still alive and if she ever thinks about me, and did she ever know how much in love with her I could have fallen.

5

**PRAISING WHAT IS LOST
MAKES THE REMEMBRANCE DEAR.**

— SHAKESPEARE

I hear Manuella downstairs coughing. She sometimes coughs in her sleep and wakes up weeping. It's going to be a trick as to which one of us goes first, me or her. Such a long life and I'm still living, which seems a miracle considering how often I've been shot, tossed from a horse, jailed, and had vengeance sworn against me. I reckon Brady's kin and a few others would still like to get their hands on me — so would Garrett's. But none ever will because they think I was dropped down a quick grave a long time ago by Big Casino, McKinney, and Poe. Did I say it was Billy Barlow that Garrett shot? It was.

Now some fella in Hico, Texas, is claiming he is me — Roberts something or other. Old man, old as me. I'll be a son of a bitch. Read about it in the *Times*. But then, he's not the first, he's just the latest. Everyone wants to be me; every few years a new me comes out of the woodwork.

34

They wouldn't if they knew what ten sorts of hell I've had to go through. I don't know what's wrong with some people.

I go down and find her sitting there at the kitchen table staring at birds. Little blue and yellow porcelain birds she's collected over the years and keeps on a shelf over the sink. She has a cup of coffee with a spoon handle sticking out. Two teaspoons of sugar, that's all she puts in her coffee. No cream. Then like as not she will dip slices of bread in it and that will be her breakfast. Bread and coffee. I don't know how she survives.

I go to her and put my hand on her shoulder, she's all bones under her housedress. Bones and skin. Can't weigh more than eighty pounds wet, I bet. I leave my hand on her shoulder until she turns her eyes away from the birds and looks at me.

"I was just sitting here thinking about Charlie and Tom and some of the others," she says.

"Why on earth for?"

I see the brown eyes Charlie saw on mornings just like this when the light comes through the window clean and bright and lights up her face.

She shrugs the shoulder I'm holding, it rises and falls like a single breath.

"I don't know why I was," she says, "I just was. Don't you ever think about them?"

Of course, but what good does it do? But I don't say this. Instead, I say:

"I thought about Tom just last week. He was a good singer. I ever tell you that?"

"Yes, and that you used to play the piano at McSween's. Charlie would say how you and Mr. McSween's wife would sit together on the bench and the two of you would play the piano — you the right hand, she the left. How come you never played for me?"

"Susan," I say, "that was her name. I wasn't all that good at it is the only reason I can think."

Her mind drifts. Mine too, but not in the same way. She claims the dead come and talk to her there at the kitchen table after I'm in bed at night. She tells it like it is real, says that Charlie sometimes comes to visit her and they talk. Maybe in her mind it is real. I say, rest in peace to those who have gone over. Even Garrett.

"What were you thinking about Charlie?" I ask, knowing that she wants me to.

"How he was my first true love," she says.

She takes a slice of bread and dips it in her coffee and chews it down, then dips some more until it is all gone. Drops of brown coffee cling to her lips.

The only picture I see of Charlie now is the one she still keeps on the bureau in the parlor. Charlie posed, sitting with a long-barreled Winchester across his knee and two bullet belts and death in his eyes. She is standing next to him, dark and pretty with black hair, her hand on his shoulder as if to say, "I'm behind you, Charlie, all the way."

I used to wonder in what ways she compared the two of us in pleasuring her and if they sat and talked at night or laid in the bed and talked after making love and what they whispered to each other, and did she still love him even though he was dead. I wondered if she took up with me because I'd offered her to, or because she really wanted to. But I don't think about those things now, haven't in years. I used to get hot thinking about it, her and Charlie together, but after a certain time of being with someone you let go of questions like that.

She spills some of her coffee into the saucer and drinks it that way, blowing on it with her lips drawn tight as a purse, then sips and stares at her birds. She's always had a fondness for birds. I remember her and Charlie had a pet crow when they were together. It had a busted wing Charlie fixed, and even after the wing healed it stayed around and she would feed it pieces of bread and it would hop up on her shoulder and stay there while she walked around the yard. She claimed it could talk, but I never heard it say anything.

I have to laugh about that because one day it got caught by the cat and the cat killed it. She cried and I said jokingly, trying to cheer her up, "Manuella, if that crow really could talk why didn't it yell for reinforcements when it saw that cat coming?"

She didn't think it was funny and didn't speak to me for a month and Charlie acted sore toward me for hurting her feelings. I guess it was pretty wrong of me to say what I did and ever after I've been careful of what I say to her about certain things. Sometimes I think she still holds it against me more than Garrett for what happened to Charlie.

"You still love Charlie?" I ask her, not knowing why except maybe just for the conversation.

Without looking away from her birds she says, "Charlie was always good to me, Henry, you know that. He was my first love. A woman doesn't just forget her first love."

"I know he was," I say. "So I guess that means you still love him."

"Not in the same way I once did, if that's what you mean."

"Do you love me, Manuella?"

She blinks and her eyes go from the birds to me. The centers are a milky blue.

"Not in the same way I loved Charlie, if that's what you mean, Henry."

"I know," I say. "I guess there's no way you could."

I think of her and Charlie on their wedding day, him loaded for bear, and think of the warm nights they spent together, her flesh still firm and her eyes still clear, and how I'd liked to have known her before he did.

She reaches up and takes hold of the hand I'm holding her shoulder with and squeezes it.

"We've had an okay life together, Henry, why bring all this up now?"

I didn't know why now, except that most of my time lately I've been spending back in the old days when we were all young and alive and full of it. I hear the guitars playing, just as she must hear Charlie's voice, and see myself dancing with senoritas and racing my horse over the sand-brown hills. I see us lying on a riverbank looking up at clouds, the blue sky, Tom, Charlie, and me. I miss it all so terribly at times that all I can do is remember and remember and remember.

I walk out on the porch, leaving her there at the table with her coffee and bread and birds. I find a place to sit where the sun is warm because my limbs are always cold even on the warmest days. In a few minutes of resting I'm right back to thinking about those days. They seemed to have lasted only a second. My whole life gone, just like that.

Tom was killed five days before Christmas by the hand of Garrett, Charlie three days later, also by Garrett. It was a sad time all the way around.

Garrett and his bunch killed more of us than we ever did of them.

So tell me who dances with blood on their hands if not Garrett and his bunch?

Sweet bird sings amid the vines
Sound of thunder deep within
The heart of fury, I weep, I weep
For what I had and lost, for lips
Unkissed, horses never rode, and
A woman's heart not yet won.

6

**THERE IS NO GREATER SORROW THAN TO
RECALL A TIME OF HAPPINESS IN MISERY.**
                                    —DANTE

Three children, all dead. The twins, Little Joe
and Catherine, named after brother and mother,
born dead. The midwife showed them to me
wrapped in a Mexican blanket. Little bloodless
things, their eyes closed, their fists balled up.
She'd washed them with a cloth before she
handed them to me. They were cold when I
touched them. Maria wanted to see but I said
no. Then she wept and said, "They're mine too,
Billy," and I said okay and had the midwife show
them to her. She held them for hours. I sat outside with Charlie and Tom and we smoked cigarettes and watched the sun cross the sky from
east to west without saying anything. Charlie
produced a bottle of Mexican Mustang Lini-
ment and we commenced to drinking. Finally
the midwife stepped out on the porch where we
were drinking and smoking and said, "Billy, you
must come help me get the babies."

Charlie volunteered, but I said no, they were mine and I'd do it.

Maria shook her head when I went to take them and held tightly the bundles they made in their little red and black blankets.

"It's time" is all I said, and took them one by one and handed them to the midwife, then sat with Maria and held her face in my hands and felt her tears spill over my fingers as her whole body shook until she fell asleep exhausted from her dreams of ruin.

Tom held one and Charlie held the other while I dug two small graves. Later we rode into Mesilla and commenced to drinking heavily until thoroughly drunk. It was the only way I knew to get the sight of those babies out of my mind.

Billito was born to me and a woman lived near Sunnyside. I know she wouldn't want me to say her name since she married a successful rancher and is still alive today. She said at the time the child should have my name because by then my name was being spoken on the lips of almost everyone in the villages and towns.

"I want him to be proud of his father — a little Billito," she said. "I want him to have your name, Billy." She was a few years older than me and had been married once but her man had gone off to search for gold and never came back. She had very sad eyes and a pretty face so I agreed to do whatever would make her happy.

41

Sometimes I would wake up next to her and think she was too old for me. She slept with her mouth open.

Billito was killed by a snake, a big rattler that bit him on the face when he was crawling around in some junk that the woman's uncle kept out behind the house, some wagon wheels and broken pots and things.

He cried and she heard him. I was on the Llano Estacado at the time with Tom and Charlie and some others running a nice fat herd of stolen Chisum cattle, taking them to Tascosa to sell to a man we knew there who didn't mind buying stolen beef. After we sold him the cattle we stole a few horses and drove them to White Oaks and sold them and I bought a new rifle and Charlie bought a new hat. Tom paid five dollars for a woman and spent the night with her. He said she didn't compare to Rose, the first whore he ever had — the one he went broke paying for her affection.

When I returned to Billito's mother she told me what had happened and where they'd buried him. The grave was already two months old by the time I got back there — just a hollow spot in the ground and a white wood cross with ribbons fluttering from it. Her uncle had made the cross and burned the boy's name into it — *Billito Bonney* — with a running iron.

"I heard him crying and found him sitting there," she said. "The snake was coiled next to him shaking its tail. He had two drops of blood like rubies on his cheek where the snake had bitten him. Silvero killed the devil with a hoe, but it was too late, too late. Billito died during the night and we buried him under the first light of morning. Jose Morales built him a small coffin out of a peach crate and Luna stitched him a suit of clothes."

It broke my interest in her and I didn't stay with her anymore after that. She later married a man who was twenty years older than her and they moved to Colorado where I hear they are quite successful.

I believe my stain was on those children and that is why they did not live. The Bible says that the children will suffer the sins of their fathers. I think that is what happened and why none of them made it — they suffered my sins.

The sun is warm on my neck and inside I hear Manuella coughing, knowing that her first love was Charlie. I know she is probably talking to him right now. He is probably sitting there at the table with her and they are talking about things I wouldn't want to hear. Things like the way his hands felt on her belly, the sweetness of her mouth, the way her breasts looked in the moon's light, maybe even the way he took two bullets from Garrett for me at Stinking Springs. He probably blames me for his death and because of it she does not forgive me and never will.

Wrapped within the pleasure is heartache.

I don't want to think of these things:
The silence of infants.
Billito bitten by a coiled snake.
Charlie and Manuella under the moon.
The stain of my sins upon my dead children.

7

**FOR GOD'S SAKE, LET US SIT UPON THE
  GROUND
AND TELL SAD STORIES OF THE DEATH
  OF KINGS:
HOW SOME HAVE BEEN DEPOSED,
  SOME SLAIN IN WAR,
SOME HAUNTED BY THE GHOSTS THEY
  HAVE DEPOSED,
SOME POISONED BY THEIR WIVES,
  SOME SLEEPING KILLED;
ALL MURDERED.**

— SHAKESPEARE

February. Cold wind. Tunstall said we should head north to Lincoln, settle the matter of the horses. We ate beans, drank down hot coffee. Brewer said, "Goddamn, she's cold," as we threw blankets and saddles on our horses.

Tunstall didn't seem to fit this country. He had sad eyes, a soft voice — some of the men called him "sister" behind his back. He was always good to me. Lent me books to read, told me I'd have a future if I could just look ahead far enough. I liked him, but he didn't look like he fit this country.

Hills like sombreros. Cottonwoods bare, tall, leaning into the wind. We took the horses along the road toward Rio Hondo to where it joined the main road from Roswell, then on to Lincoln near Tinnie.

Tunstall rode out front, casual, unconcerned. He was wearing a long black coat and a fancy hat with a brim wide as a dinner plate, kid gloves, trousers stuffed into the tops of his riding boots.

Waite was driving a buckboard. We left him going up the road so's we could take a shortcut, climbing up the west side of the Pajaritos. It was slow going on account of the herd of horses we were driving. We rode all day under the arc of a winter sun. Reached a canyon we had to run through in order to get to Ruidoso, four, five miles distant yet.

That's when we kicked up the flock of wild turkeys. Naturally we wanted to bag a few, so we set chase after them. Tunstall shouted he'd stay with the herd.

Billy Morton, Tom Hill, Frank Baker, Jesse Evans. They killed Tunstall. Them and the others, twenty or thirty in all. Some of us had gone on ahead, chasing the wild turkeys up a hill. Brewer heard the pounding hooves coming up from behind us. Then a bullet snapped a twig over our heads and another and another like a swarm of bees, and we knew we were in for it.

46

Poor Tunstall down below in the canyon alone, not even armed. That's what brave men they were. Morton, Hill, Baker, Jess Evans, and that whole bunch.

We could see some of it from in the rocks. It happened quick. Tunstall turned his horse back around to face them. Billy Morton rode up and shot him in the face, then some others fired into his body as he lay upon the ground. I saw with my own eyes Evans get off his horse and smash in Tunstall's head with his rifle stock. For sport they shot his horse.

Brewer said, "Jesus Christ!"

That wasn't enough. They laid Tunstall next to his horse, side by side, then took his coat and put it under his head and his hat under the horse's like they were resting. Like they had stopped along the trail to take a nap. Goddamn sons of bitches! Laughing all the time. Big joke, killing an unarmed man as easy-mannered as Tunstall was. No courage in that and no heart in any of them. If they died the way they lived, then who is to say that justice was not served? We could have faced them up, the four of us, but we would have ended up just as dead as John, and we knew it. Four or five of them to each one of us. Even a bulldog knows when it's licked and they had us licked that day.

I had my own plans for Morton, Hill, Baker, and Evans. I figured to give them the same chance they gave Tunstall. None at all. And that's exactly what I gave them. None at all.

That night we told the story of what happened while standing in the saloon in Lincoln. Cold night, lights dim, shadows of men along the wall, along the bar — hard to tell friend from foe. But wasn't any of us cared right then all that much. We were ready for a fight, still full of outrage about Tunstall. And maybe just as much outraged about our own inability to do anything about it.

"You reckon we shoulda fought them?" Widenmann said.

"Hell yes, we should have," I said.

"Naw," Middleton said. "What could we have done but git ourselves kilt too?"

"Maybe it ain't finished yet," I said.

"It's a hell of a thing what they did," Widenmann said.

"Buncha dirty bastards," Middleton said.

"I know every one of them," I said. "It's not finished. I don't forget."

"Let it go," Brewer said.

"Fuck you, Dick."

He looked at me hard. We both knew something we weren't saying.

Later, two, three in the morning, I woke up from a dream, my heart beating fast. The room was cold and when I looked out the window there was snow on the ground and I thought of Tunstall, lying out there with the snow covering him. It was the loneliest thought I ever had.

Celsa awoke when I tripped over a chair in the dark and fell.

"Billy?" is all she said and held out her arms and I got in the bed with her and let her hold me.

"What's wrong, Billy?" she said after holding me for a while. I was shivering and didn't realize it.

"I guess I'm going to have to kill Morton and some of the others," I said, "for what they done to John. I know all those boys and like most of them, but I can't help wanting to kill them now."

I could feel her warmth, see by the wan light of the moon that fell through the window, her small brown figure. She was like sugar to me. In the moonlight her hair was black as crow feathers. She had small breasts as sweet as prickly pear fruit and I loved to hold them and taste them. She was more like a girl than a woman. Here in the cold her body was a fire against my skin. Hot and comforting in a way I'd come to depend on. I thought of John Tunstall, his cold body lying lonely where we'd left him. It gnawed at me, the thought we'd left him and run like cowards. I kissed Celsa harshly and she pulled back, a drop of blood on her lip.

"Billy . . ."

I didn't realize how hard I'd kissed her.

"I'm sorry," I said. "I didn't mean it."

She took my face in her hands.

"Es all right, mi querido," she said.

I kissed her again, more gently this time.

49

The next day several of us took a wagon out and got Tunstall's body. He was stiff when we picked him up, whether from the cold or death I couldn't say. We brushed the snow off him and picked him up, me at his feet, and laid him in the back of the springboard wagon we borrowed from Wilson. Dick sat in the seat and drove while me and George Middleton rode behind, our rifles at the ready across our pommels. Crows were perched on Tunstall's horse and flew off when we first got there. Dick shot one of them with his pistol, its body black against the snow, dripping a fresh ribbon of blood. Tunstall's hands and face were pecked red.

We buried him near the banks of the Bonito where the river runs quiet, next to the graves of two unnamed children. The lot belonged to McSween, the dead children to Salazar. McSween was going to have a school built on the lot, but the way it turned out the dead needed the earth more than the living.

The little wooden crosses of the dead children stood at angles, leaning away from the wind. I guess if you had stood up on one of the nearby hills and looked down at us, it might have looked like a gathering of crows, all the men and women dressed in mourner's black. I wore what I had: rough coat, heavy brown sweater, long scarf, ribbed trousers, gloves, and a hat. I guessed Tunstall wouldn't have minded I owned no funeral clothes — he wouldn't have been counting on any of us going to a funeral so soon. Especially his.

All in all a cold day, but with the sun at our backs. Tom sang a hymn. I can't remember exactly which, but his voice was pleasing and some of the women wept. Doc Easly performed the service. The only words I remember were these: "If a man die, so shall he live again." It struck me as an odd thought.

There we stood, every one of us except for McSween, Ealy, and the women armed to the teeth, the wind snatching at the women's dresses, trying to tug the hats off our heads. Sheriff Brady wouldn't arrest the guilty but sent for a detachment of soldiers from Fort Stanton to make sure we didn't start war that day. I put him on my list. He was in Murphy and Dolan's pocket deep as a silver dollar and I put him on my list along with Morton, Hill, Baker, Evans, and the rest. He looked at me across the grave with yellow wolf eyes, his hands balled into fists like he was too damn good to die, but I had news for him.

When it was over a small group of Mexican musicians with brass horns and guitars played a mournful dirge, which got the women crying all the harder and caused some of the men to blink and look off toward the hills like the wind had gotten something in their eyes. All I could feel was anger.

Later we went to McSween's and held a big powwow and ate and talked about war against

51

Murphy and Dolan.

Later still Susan McSween and I played the piano in the parlor of the McSween home — the only piano in Lincoln County as far as I know. It was a bright cheery room with wallpaper that had small blue flowers printed on it. There were several photographs in black oval frames hanging on the walls and muslin curtains drawn back from the windows. The piano itself was of a dark wood with carved legs and atop it sat a silver music stand and a pair of silver candlesticks.

I sat on the bench alongside her while her long fingers spanned the keys, darting like butterflies. The others stood or sat around in overstuffed chairs and on a horsehair settee. Brewer stared out the window like he'd lost something he wasn't ever going to get back. Alex McSween talked to Widenmann and a few of the others, plotting strategy.

Then, in the middle of a song, Mrs. McSween's fingers brushed over mine and we looked at each other without saying a thing, but something strong passed between us. We were playing one of my favorites, "Silver Threads Among the Gold."

I guess we all had a loneliness in us, and it wasn't just from the land or from the killings or from any one place — but the loneliness came from a lot of different places all at once and gathered in us at unexpected times.

I felt my blood stir when her fingers touched mine.

Then McSween said, "Susan, what a lovely song," and came over and stood next to the piano and I felt all wrong inside for thinking what I'd been thinking.

Being there in that place, the McSweens' home, made me realize how little I had, how little I wanted from life. Until that moment I never thought much about anything except staying alive, dancing, spending my nights with this senorita or that. A boy like me wasn't ever given much to live for in the first place. I thought about the father I never knew, the one I did know. I thought about my mother, about the first man I killed, how things had come to me in hard ways. And look at me now, losing again someone I cared about — Tunstall — the one some of the others called "sister" but to me a friend.

I guess if I could have had anything right at that moment it would have been a regular life. A woman like Susan McSween for my wife, a warm home, a piano. Those are the things I'd have wanted. But I knew it wasn't in the cards and wasn't ever going to be in the cards. I think if Tunstall had lived, had stayed my friend, I might have stood a decent chance. But as it was, with him in the ground, I just couldn't see how I was going to come out of any of this any good.

"Would you like to play another?" Susan McSween said.

I looked deeply into her green eyes.

"I guess not," I said, and went out into the

cold day and walked some distance away from the house. And when I looked back I could see movement in the windows and I thought to myself:

They're in there and I'm out here and that's the way it's always going to be.

I could just ride away.

I could go back east, try to make something out of my life.

Or I could stay and take care of the dirty business fate had given me.

Goddamn you, Brady and Morton and all the rest, for what you've done. I'll see you in hell or I won't see you at all.

A crow flew low, cawing as it went, cawing my name across the sky. I watched until it became a black dot.

That night I slept in Celsa's bed and thought of Susan McSween, how her fingers had brushed mine playing the piano and the look she gave me and I her. I reached for Celsa and drew her near, trying to block out the thoughts I was having. Events were moving too fast for me to sleep. Tunstall lying stiff with snow. McSween talking war while his wife's hand brushed mine. Celsa's slow breath against my face.

"Celsa," I whispered, and when she stirred I pushed up her nightgown.

Let me tell you, this was the beginning of future sorrows.

8

**ALL LOSSES ARE RESTOR'D AND
SORROWS END.**

— SHAKESPEARE

After Garrett killed me, I headed south, across
the Rio Grande. All my pals murdered, it was
time to think about my future. Wallace fell
through on his promise to pardon me — that was
the first thing — and the Santa Fe Ring was out
for my skin. Too many enemies, not enough
friends. Hell, it didn't take a Republican to figure it out.

I rode south for two days, camped near
streams, and made cold camps. A woman I knew
in Tularosa had taught me to read the stars:
Orion, the Big and Little Dippers, the Archer. At
night I'd lie on my blanket with my head on my
saddle, staring at the sky, seeing how many stars
I could name. The same woman read the bumps
on my head to determine my character. She said
I was destined to become a wealthy politician. I
laughed till I cried.

I made my way to El Caballo where I knew

some people. Ol' man Garza was the first to spot
me. He had eyes like a water dog, a face of folded
brown wrinkles, and walked stooped over.
"Billy, where are your companeros?" he said.
Tom and Charlie and me had gone there a few
times together. Tom had a girlfriend there, a
mestizo.

"All dead," I said. "Killed." He shook his
head, hair white as goose feathers.

"How is it they didn't kill you too, amigo?" he
said.

"I'm just lucky," I said. "Always have been."

We sat and drank a little mescal from an olla
he had kept in the shade of his jacal and watched
two dogs humping.

"Tom too?" he said, after we each took a
drink. "The one with the red hair?"

"Tom was the first," I said. "Killed by the law,
shot through the guts."

"Ayie, that's too bad. Ysidra will be disappointed. Every day she watches the north road to
see if he is coming back to her."

"She will have a long wait," I said.

We drank and his old woman brought us some
frijoles and chilies and we ate them, then I went
to the adobe where Tom's girlfriend lived.

She had coarse black hair and wasn't as pretty
as most of the girls I took to.

She looked past me, saw that I was alone.

"Tomasito?" she said in Spanish. Tom didn't
know a single word of Mex but I could speak it
like a native. He rarely spoke of her unless we

were spending the night in the village. He had a regular girlfriend he wrote letters to back in Indiana. Her name was Anne. He had said he intended to marry her someday. He had a letter from her in his pocket when Garrett shot him. Buried near the Pecos in Sumner with Charlie, and now me, is as close to Indiana as Tom is ever going to get.

Every few years the Pecos floods its banks and the dead get carried away. It's the only place I know where the dead don't stay buried. I reckon Tom, Charlie, and me will end up south of the border come a big rain, floating along in our coffins pretty as you please.

I told her what had happened, saw the sad hurt creep into her eyes.

"We're both alone now, Ysidra," I said. "No reason we have to be." She understood and invited me in.

That night I made cups of my hands and held her breasts in them and touched her between her legs, and she touched me between mine under a moon that was full and bright and lit the room in silver light. Once she called me Tom, said it in a whisper. I didn't mind. Later we ate our supper sitting on the bed naked, then fell asleep in each other's arms. I woke once and she was crying. I put on my pants and went outside and smoked a cigarette and looked up at the stars. I saw the Archer clear as anything and wondered if Tom and Charlie were up there dodging his arrows or lying under the dust back in Sumner, me between them.

I stayed in that village for two or three months, drinking mescal and racing my horse with some of the men who had good horses and a few pesos to bet. Ysidra and I went for picnics and I taught her how to lasso tree stumps and fired my pistol for her at tin cans, making them jump three feet in the air with either hand, and one day she asked me if I would return to the north and avenge Tom. We made love on a blanket in the rain and once the horses ran off and we had to walk three miles back to the village. It was an easy life. I put on some weight and got my spirits back.

But I grew restless and ran low on money and the opportunities in that part of the country were poor at best. Even if I stole a cow or a horse, who was I going to sell it to, some poor Mex lucky to have a full pot of beans and a few tortillas? It was pretty enough land, but its people were as poor as sin. Rich men lived in the cities with the trash blowing down the streets and stink in the air. The poor lived where the grass was tall and the rivers ran clear.

Of all the folks I knew north of the Rio Grande there were only two alive I could trust: Sallie Chisum and Sue McSween. Both sweet gals. I could still feel the brush of Sue McSween's fingers against mine when we played the piano while her husband talked of peace. Sallie had old John, her uncle, to keep her company. But Sue was alone now just like me, McSween dead during the shootout when they burned the house with us in it. All his education and being a man of God hadn't done a thing to stop the bullets that night. One of Murphy's men walked up and emptied his revolver into McSween's chest. Bibles won't stop bullets, that's what McSween learned. His wife had the same hate for the other side I did. We understood each other in that way, maybe some other ways too. I had a strong desire to see her and that's what I did. I rode north again and saw Susan McSween.

Gone from Lincoln and the blood spilled there, Three Rivers is where I found her.

She said, "God, I'm seeing a ghost."

She pinched my cheeks and I gave her a big foolish grin.

She took hold of me and pressed me close, then stepped back and said, "But Garrett killed you in Fort Sumner. That's the word. When I heard, I thought, 'They have killed the last one.' "

She made us a pot of tea and we sat on the east porch and stared off toward the Sierra Blancas, my little horse tied to a mimosa tree, its chest lathered with sweat.

"You look thin," she said.

"I'm fat and sassy," I said. I put three sugar cubes in my tea.

"If Garrett or the others find you . . ."

"I don't think Garrett is looking too hard," I said. "He's looking harder for that reward than he ever did for me."

"If it wasn't you at Maxwell's that night, then who?"

"Billy Barlow, is the way I heard it. He was staying with a Mexican woman, went into Pete's that night, that's all I know."

"I dream of Alex almost every night still," she said, the brown ringlets of her hair touching her cheeks. "Like he is still with us."

"Your husband was a good soul who put too much trust in God and the wrong men," I said. "Him and John both. I don't think God himself would set foot in Lincoln County. And I think if he did they'd kill him too."

"They said you killed Sheriff Brady and the men who killed John Tunstall. They are laying murders on your head all up and down the Pecos and Rio Hondo, Billy. Every day for a time I read where you killed this person or that. Then I heard Garrett killed you at Fort Sumner and thought, 'That's the last of it.' Now here you are big as life."

"This is good tea" was all I said to her about that business. I think she understood, for she asked if I still sang and played the piano and I was glad she changed the subject.

"I'd like it if you didn't say anything about me still breathing," I said.

"Understood. I won't say a word. But you know you can't stay long in this country or someone will find you out." Her eyes were dark as chestnuts after a rain.

"I know."

"I have some money," she said. "It would be a start."

"I couldn't take any."

"Don't be foolish. After what you did for us."

She reached out and patted my hand and let hers rest there for a few moments but it wasn't the same as before, that time playing the piano. Something had changed and dampened our spirits.

"Alex would want me to stake you," she said after a little more time had passed.

"I'll consider it a loan if you do," I said. And that's how it worked out. She gave me eight hundred dollars with the promise that I would abandon the territory and use the money for a fresh start. I repaid her every last dime and signed my name Joe Miller each time, but she had to know who it was from.

That evening before I left we played the piano. She kissed me on the cheek and squeezed my hands.

"I'm glad they didn't kill you, Billy. Run and don't ever come back. Promise me that."

I heard she died last year in White Oaks an old woman. A man from Tularosa came and bought her piano at auction. I would have gone to the funeral if I'd known in time. She was a good gal and didn't deserve the hand dealt to her. None of us did, but that's all water under the bridge.

I'll probably be joining her soon. Her and the others. Tom, Charlie, even old Garrett, all of us floating down the Pecos the next big flood. Hell, it truly is something that I outlasted all of them. It says in the Bible, the last shall be first and the first shall be last. I guess that makes me first, for all the rest are gone.

I close my eyes to the dappling sun filtering through the chinaberry trees. I still can hear her playing "Silver Threads Among the Gold" as her fingers brush over the keys and over mine, our voices rising together above the flames. That night I killed several and was shot in the doing.

9

**TO WITHDRAW IS NOT TO RUN AWAY,
AND TO
STAY IS NO WISE ACTION, WHEN THERE'S
MORE
REASON TO FEAR THAN TO HOPE.**
— **CERVANTES**

John Chisum, hawk face, fierce eyes, but yellow inside when it came to doing his own fighting. Had himself a nigger named Abe Lincoln Washington who carried a Sharps Big Fifty. Shooting cattle rustlers was what Chisum paid him for. Hunt them like coyotes and shoot them with that Big Fifty. Shoot them in the head, in the spine, in the heart, didn't matter. Shoot them and leave them lying where they fell, then move on in search of another. Rotting corpses and bleached bones, testimony to all who would steal John's ten-dollar cows.

All the boys were afraid of that black getting after them with his big buffalo gun. Said he hunted you at night so you could not see him. You'd be asleep in your bedroll and hear a big roar like thunder rolling across the hills and know it was the nigger out there in the dark hunting cattle thieves.

I wanted to ride up and get some of Chisum's cattle and take them to Tascosa but the boys were worried about getting shot like coyotes. This was before Charlie took up with us. Charlie was recently married and was trying to farm near the Rio Bonito with Manuella in those days. Sometimes he'd get out of bed and ride over and steal a few cows with us, but mostly he liked what he referred to as "sleeping in."

Our bunch was made up of Billy Morton, Jesse Evans, Billy Campbell, Vincente Romero, Chavez, Morris, Tom, and myself. Of course this was before they murdered Tunstall and put bad blood between us. Until then we all were of the same mind: steal Chisum's fat cattle and drive them across the border and onto the Llano and sell them. And afterward get drunk, raise quite a bit of hell, then steal some horses to bring back. We were wild boys.

"I'll kill that dirty black son of a bitch!" Jess said, his belly full of mescal and beans when we talked about Abe Lincoln Washington that particular night, the camp's fire eating a hole in the darkness.

Jess had a big bold mouth and a mean nature to go with it. And he later told a lot of lies about the night he murdered Susan McSween's lawyer, Chapman, on the streets of Lincoln. One lie he told was about how he held a gun to my

64

head and dared me to do something about it. Partly true, but not the way he said. But before that ever happened, we had no animosity between us.

"Go ahead," I said that night, knowing he didn't have it in him. "I'd like to see you shoot the colored hand of John's."

Some of the boys laughed and urged him on, and he did saddle a horse and ride out that night, not to return until noon the next day.

"I found him and killed him," Jess declared upon his arrival back in camp, but no one believed him when he couldn't explain where the body was.

"Ate him," Jess said after being pressed by the boys. "I roasted him over a fire and ate him. There ain't no body to be found, just some bones I threw in the creek."

We all laughed and so did Jess.

Word came down that John wanted to meet with me so I went up to his house at Seven Rivers, keeping a good vigil for the black, making myself small so a bullet wouldn't find the back of my head.

They were all there when I got there, John, Sallie, and the colored, who squatted on his heels in the yard of the longhouse.

The black was oiling that Big Fifty and had it laid across his knees. Flop hat, hands dark as walnut working a rag over the metal. Blue-black skin. Working that oil rag back and forth along the barrel.

Chisum was sitting in a ladder-back rocker, a red satin pillow under his haunches, Sallie next to him, pretty as a picture, the sunlight dancing in her yellow curls, eyes blue as pieces of the sky. "Hi, Henry," she called as soon as I rode up close enough.

"Kid," John said, "climb down, let's talk."

I did as he invited, but I kept an eye on the black, who was keeping one on me as well.

"Sal, go get Henry something cold to drink," John said, telling her how thirsty such a long ride had probably made me.

"Your man there kill any rustlers lately, Mr. Chisum?" I asked John as I took up a seat next to him. Just sitting there on that long veranda, I could almost feel rich, feel some of John's wealth rubbing off on me. Chisum ignored my comment about his man, like he did most things he didn't want to give answers to.

Sallie brought us lemonade and poured it from a china pitcher into fruit jars and handed me one, then handed one to John before pouring some for herself and sitting down next to me on my right. She was pretty and gave me a big smile.

"I had to send to Juarez for these lemons," John said, sipping and smacking his lips before licking the pulp off. I drank two jars, John three, before we got down to business.

"I want you and your pals to stop stealing my cattle," he told me. "That's what I called you out here to talk to you about. You need jobs. I got plenty that don't include running off my herds.

You like herding cows so well, you can herd them for me for wages."

I looked at Sallie and offered her a smile. She rolled her eyes without him seeing.

"John, I'd never knowingly steal a cow of yours," I told him with a straight face.

"Abraham," he called to the black man and he stood up.

"Come, bring that gun of yours and show the Kid here what you can do with it."

The colored tucked the oil rag in his back pocket getting up, then took out a bullet long as my forefinger and slipped it into the breech.

"You aiming to have him kill me, John, right here on your veranda in front of Sallie?"

"You just watch a thing or two," John said.

The black walked out in the middle of the yard and took sight down the barrel at something far into the distance. He flipped up a tang sight, then looked some more.

"What's he aiming at?" I asked, for I couldn't see a living thing in the direction he was pointing his big bore.

"A prairie dog, I suspect. They're a nuisance just like snakes and rustlers," John said. He had a sour look on his face, as if Sallie hadn't put enough sugar in the lemonade to suit him.

I strained my eyes to see a prairie dog but couldn't see one.

Then the gun roared and kicked back into the black's shoulder and a spume of bloody dust appeared five or six hundred yards in the distance, then settled to earth again.

"Now you know," John said and poured himself and me another glass of lemonade. "He don't miss and that gun of his could drop a buffalo at twice that distance if there were any buffalos still left. Just think what it can do to a man."

"Is it true," I said, "that he hunts in the dark?"

"Don't play games, Kid. This is serious business."

"What if I pull my pistol and shoot that fellow of yours, John? Would you have to send all the way to Juarez for another one like you did for these lemons?"

He looked at me then, the skin as smooth and yellow as candle wax over his bony cheeks.

"You can take your choice, Kid. Come to work for me or clear off my land."

"That's not much of a choice," I told him, but he had already started into the house, leaving Sallie and me sitting there.

"Uncle John's determined to clean up the rustling," she said. "I'm fond of you, Henry, and would not want harm to come to you. If he tells Abraham to shoot you, that is what he will do. It would break my heart to have that happen."

I thanked her for the good lemonade and kissed the knuckles on her hand, bowing low like I read Frenchmen did. She told me it made her heart beat fast and that I was the first man to ever kiss her hand that way. I could feel the blood ticking in her wrist.

"Good-bye, Sal. Don't you worry about ol' Abraham there shooting me."

I mounted my pony and rode it up close to the nigger.

"That was a good shot," I told him. "But I'm not a prairie dog."

He opened his hand and showed me the empty brass shell.

"I knows you ain't, Mr. Billy, but I do what Mr. Chisum tell me. He tell me I got to shoot you, then that's what I do."

"Then you'd better not miss."

He twisted his mouth, then put the empty cartridge in his pocket.

"I never miss what I aims for," he said.

"Neither do I."

I rode bravely off, but the whole ride back to where the gang had camped along the Rio Hondo I kept thinking about that shot he made on that prairie dog, seeing that bloody spray way off in the distance and those honest eyes of his when he said he killed whatever John told him to kill.

"Boys," I said when I rode into our camp, "I believe it's time we shook the dust from our feet and found new territory."

"You seen him, didn't you, Bill?" Tom said. "You seen that night-stalking nigger of John's."

Some of the boys looked at Jesse, who was drunk, laid out by the fire, the soles of his boots smoking.

"You see that prairie dog way out yonder?" I

said, pointing toward the slope of a hill.

Tom looked so hard he squinted his eyes.

"No. I don't see no prairie dog, Billy."

"Neither do I," I said. "But I saw John's nigger kill one just like it with a single shot."

We packed up that night and never stole another one of John Chisum's beeves. Leastways, I never did. You might say it was because I didn't want to break Sallie Chisum's pretty heart.

10

INDEED THE IDOLS I HAVE LOVED SO LONG
HAVE DONE MY CREDIT IN THIS WORLD
   MUCH WRONG:
HAVE DROWNED MY GLORY IN A SHALLOW
   CUP,
AND SOLD MY REPUTATION FOR A SONG.
                 — EDWARD FITZGERALD

Isabella was more than I ever expected. She called herself a Castilian, a Spaniard, not a Mexican. She had blue eyes, which was unusual for Mexicans but not for Spaniards, and was almost as tall as Garrett. The first time I laid eyes on her I knew she was of a different order than anything I'd ever seen before.

We were in Sonora to raise a little hell and steal cattle. Charlie, Tom, and me. Some of the others were supposed to meet us so we lazed around waiting. Tom was teaching this little black and white dog he had to stand on its hind legs by tempting it with hard candy. Charlie was writing Manuella a letter on a penny's worth of paper with a pencil he kept touching to the tip of his tongue. I wasn't doing anything but watching folks come and go, running between the raindrops. It was the season of rain and every day we had us a little storm that blew in and then blew back out again, leaving the air fresh and sweet-smelling and the sky blue as a glass jar.

Isabella arrived in a carriage pulled by matched black horses and driven by a peon wearing a white jacket and pants — an old man with gray hair thick as cotton tick. I watched him pull the rig up in front of the mercantile, step down, and come around with a parasol that he popped open and held for Isabella. He was barely tall enough to hold it over her head. As it was, she had to bend slightly.

She wore a fine green dress trimmed in black and a wide-brimmed hat of black felt ringed by ostrich feathers. The dress had a bustle in the back and I was fascinated by the way it shifted when she walked.

"You see that?" I said to Tom. He looked up and the dog fell over, a piece of hard candy in its mouth.

"See what?" he said, but by then Isabella and the peon had already entered the mercantile.

"Nothing," I said. He rolled his eyes and went back to teaching the dog tricks.

I glanced at Charlie, who had his nose near to touching the paper he was writing on, the pencil making scratching sounds as he wrote. He was so fixed on that letter you could almost see the words dripping out of his eyes.

"Tell Manuella hello for me," I said. I don't know that he even heard me.

"I think I'll go over to that mercantile and buy myself some cartridges and maybe a new bandanna," I said and trotted across the street.

I must have looked a sight: dripping wet, the brim of my hat flopped down, my boots muddy. She turned to look at me, a pair of silver spurs in her hand. The merchant knew me from times before and spoke and spoke my name when he saw me walk through the door. His was Octavio. I greeted him with a swoop of my hat but my eyes never left her the whole time. She took her time about doing it, but she turned her attention from me back to the silver spurs, which she studied for a moment longer before handing them to Octavio.

"I will take these," she said. "And the saddle too."

There was a fancy saddle with hand-tooling hanging from the wall above the counter.

"Those are mighty large spurs for a lady," I said.

She turned to look at me again, the peon with her, unhappy that I had spoken, his eyes fixed on me with a warning look.

"Rodrigo," she said, "take the saddle and put it in the carriage," and he did.

I walked to the counter and took up one of the spurs and examined it, then set it down again. I could hear the rustle of her dress each time she moved and smell the soft sweet scent of her skin, see the ticking of her heart along the curve of her neck.

"They are not for me, senor," she said. "They are for my father. It is his birthday."

"He is a lucky man," I said. "For tonight he will have these fancy spurs and that handsome saddle, but more than that he has a beautiful daughter."

My attempt to charm her seemed wasted for she didn't even blink at my compliment.

"Are you a flatterer by nature?" she said.

Maybe she didn't blush, but I did; I felt a little bowled over by her.

"I believe in saying what's on my mind," I said. "Do you blame me for that?"

"No, I do not blame you for that." She spoke to Octavio in Spanish, probably thinking I wouldn't understand, but I understood.

"This young man," she said. "Do you know him well?"

"Si. He is Billito Bonney from north of the Rio Grande. A boy who the girls all love to dance with, always playing jokes on his friends, a generous boy of good nature."

I played dumb, like I didn't know what they'd said, though Octavio knew I talked the lingo as well as any native.

She turned her attention back to me then and said, "Senor Octavio tells me that you enjoy dancing. Is it true?"

"About as well as anything," I said, "and better than most things. I hear music, my feet just naturally get to moving."

"We are having a fiesta for my father this evening. You are invited to come."

"I am with friends," I said.

"Good. You can bring them along if you wish."

She gave me directions to her ranchero, then I watched her go through the rain protected by the parasol her peon held for her. I watched them ride away in her fancy carriage, its wheels slathering through the mud, the scent of her still lingering in the air.

Charlie looked glum by the time I rejoined him and Tom.

"I miss Manuella," he said. "What am I doing so far from home?"

"I think poor Charlie is blue," Tom said, hoisting the dog onto his shoulder. "Let's go have a whiskey and cheer him up."

"Whiskey and a bath, boys," I said. "Tonight we're going to a baile."

"Not me," Charlie said, folding his letter and putting it away in his vest pocket. "Manuella wouldn't have it, me dancing with other women." I think about it now, all these years later, and see how much she was jealous and in love with him, how he adored her to the point he wouldn't even dance with another woman, and I am filled with some strange regret.

"You think she can see all the way from the Rio Hondo to Mexico to see what it is you're doing?" Tom said. Tom's eyes were wide with mocking.

75

"No, but she'd know the minute I got home," Charlie said.

"I'd like to dance with a fat girl," Tom said. "A big brown senorita I could squeeze up against her pillows."

"You can have my share," Charlie said. "Two fat girls if that's what you want because I ain't going."

I could hear the music playing already in my heart and feel Isabella dancing in my arms. I could taste her breath sweet against my face under a sky of stars and crimson shadows.

Two young heifers roasting over glowing beds of coals, young men, their faces red from the heat, their hands constantly turning the spitted meat, were the first things Tom and me saw when we arrived at the ranchero. There was a courtyard of cobbled stone and smooth tile with an arched entry and a fountain where water gurgled from a stone horse's mouth. Luminaries lighted the walks and were strung in trees, the yellow flickering candlelight winking inside the glass bowls like a hundred happy eyes. Music from the big guitars and the brass horns of the marachi lifted into the deep velvet air. The musicians were dressed in large sombreros stitched with silver threads and had conchos sewn along the seams of their trousers. Most had round bellies that protruded from their fancy jackets. Tom and me wore red silk scarves around our necks, ones I'd purchased from Octavio.

Isabella saw us at the same instant I saw her and came immediately toward us, as if she had been waiting for our arrival. She wore a dress that was such a creamy white that it made it impossible not to notice her. I was glad I'd shined myself up some and put on a clean shirt and scraped the dirt from under my fingernails and borrowed some of Charlie's bay rum for my hair.

Isabella welcomed us and I introduced Tom and he bowed and said, "Pleased to meet you," and it caused her to smile for the first time because he bowed just like a prince.

"Do you care to demonstrate your skills with a dance?" she said. I offered her my arm and soon we were dancing to the lively music, my heels clicking on the stone, Isabella twirling just as I'd imagined ever since the moment I saw her with silver spurs.

It seemed to me the beginning of a new life: Isabella in her white dress, the strum of guitars, the hacienda twinkling in the night like stars fallen to earth, tables laden with food and drink, gay laughter and a million acres of lowing cattle. I thought of how wonderful it would be never having to get my feet wet crossing the Rio Grande again. It was easy temptation and especially so when I looked into the face of this beautiful woman. For all I could see that night was Isabella. And all I knew was that every time I looked at her it took my breath away.

Nothing could have foretold the events to

come — killing Brady and Ollinger and Bell and the others, the trial and the death sentence they hung on me, Garrett's deceit, the murders of Charlie and Tom, and all the rest of what was to occur in those coming days. Seems sorrow and bitterness trailed me all the days of my life, and the best times, like that night, came rare as desert rain.

I looked into her eyes and became lost.

I looked into her eyes and was found.

For she made my heart tender and made me wish for better things for myself.

This they never told about me.

11

A GIRL ROSE THAT HAD RED MOURNFUL
   LIPS
AND SEEMED THE GREATNESS OF THE
   WORLD IN TEARS,
AROSE, AND ON THE INSTANT CLAMOROUS
   EAVES,
A CLIMBING MOON UPON AN EMPTY SKY,
AND ALL THAT LAMENTATION OF THE
   LEAVES,
COULD BUT COMPOSE MAN'S IMAGE AND
   HIS CRY.

                      — W. B. YEATS

Silver City. Nothing silver about it except the sky late in the day when the shadows grow long on the streets and the silver that men put in their heads hoping to strike it rich, like Antrim did with Mother.

Antrim began showing up regular before any of us knew it. Thin man with chin whiskers like a goat sitting at our table, knife in one hand, fork in the other, his eager eyes all over Mother and the platter of pork and the sweet potatoes like they were all one and the same to him. Joe said he didn't like it, the way Antrim looked at Mother. I didn't like it either, but she didn't seem to mind. Mother's gray-blue eyes would steal glances at him and he'd curl his lips back and show his horsey teeth to her, the pork grease slick in his whiskers. When they first started going for walks after supper, the leaves of the cottonwoods were just turning brittle and he had taken to calling her by her first name and she his. Catherine and William.

Joe said he wished Antrim would ride off but we both knew he wasn't going to any more than he was going to stop showing up for supper with his eating utensils in his shirt pocket. He was like a dog set on a rabbit's trail and wasn't about to quit before he got her.

"Damn it, Henry, what are we going to do?" Joe would say, the skin just below his right eye ticking like a heartbeat. Joe could get hot fast.

"Nothing we can do," I said, because as far as I could see, there wasn't. Me but fifteen and scrawny as a starved cat and Joe but two years older and not much bigger.

"I ought to whip him."

"I'll help you."

Joe looked at me and shook his head and laughed.

"You'd help me jump on a pole cat, wouldn't you, Henry?"

We stood as witnesses for Mother while she and Antrim were married. That night me and

Joe noticed how he slipped into her bedroom, his boots in his hands like a thief getting ready to steal something that wasn't his. Me and Joe slept in the yard under a chinaberry tree and the rain soaked our clothes but still, we didn't set foot back in the house that night and took regular to sleeping out of doors until it turned too cold. Having Antrim around made us feel guilty about staying in our own home.

It wasn't long after that my schoolmates began calling me Kid Antrim. I whipped plenty of them when they did. And the old man whipped me and Joe plenty whenever we got in dutch with him, which could be over almost anything. Mother had that hurt look whenever Antrim would lay into us with his belt, but men who would take up with a widow and two wild boys were at a dear price in that country so she didn't interfere with his *educating* us.

I think Antrim brought her the lung fever. He had it in him, then passed it to her, and she got sick with it and coughed up blood into her hanky and began to grow as thin as he was. Then thinner.

Her last day she called me to her room where she lay under a thick quilt of faded blue patches and white squares, her hair loose and fanned out in a yellow spider's web on the pillow. Her skin had turned the hue of tallow by this time, her eyes as faded as the blue patches of her quilt. I could smell her sickness in the air and on her nightstand was a tin pan awash in bloody flux.

She looked to me to be as frail as a wounded bird.

"Come closer to me, Henry, and let me look at you."

I leaned near and felt her fever hot against my face. Like heat off a stove lid.

She looked at me a long time, as if she was seeing me for the first time, but really it was the last and she knew it long before any of us. Antrim sat in the corner watching her watching me and didn't say a word. There was the heavy scent of coal oil in the room along with the sour way he smelled, and Mother's sickness. It was a room whose smell I will always remember.

"I want you and Joe to be good boys and listen to Mister," she said, meaning Antrim. "He's promised to take care of you both until you're old enough to be on your own. For that I thank the gracious God in Heaven. To think that my boys would be left orphans . . ." She took in a sharp breath, then coughed, and I held the pan for her until she could catch her breath and lean back again.

I pressed my thumbs to the corners of her eyes and daubed away the tears that lingered there as warm as summer rain.

"Henry, promise to be a good boy now."

"I promise."

She took her fingers and pressed them to her lips, then to mine, while Antrim looked on in cold silence, his eyes narrow with hatred, I suppose for the way she was dying and saddling him with Joe and me. He hadn't bargained for whelps the first time he sat at our table and assessed his position in our little family.

"Good," she said, "go tell Joe I want to see him." And when I did is when she died — in those few moments, before I could even say good-bye to her.

"I don't want to go in there and see her that way," Joe said. But finally I talked him into it.

Antrim had pulled the quilt up over her face and Joe pulled it down and looked at her a long time, then at him and said, "You don't have any right," and I thought Antrim would slip loose his belt and lay into him with it but instead he simply walked out of the room, his bony hands balled into fists.

"She's gone," Joe said after a long time of looking at her.

"I know she is."

"What now, Henry? She's gone, what now?"

Ten days later I was locked up in the jail for stealing a Chinaman's clothes, a crime committed by Sombrero Jack but guess who got the donkey's tail pinned on him.

Hell, I knew as I was climbing out the chimney making my jailbreak I wasn't ever coming back to Silver City, except maybe in a pine box.

There was no silver in Silver City. No silver lining either. And what I learned was, a man makes his own silver just as he makes his own tin.

Antrim I shall never forgive for giving Mother

her lung fever. I don't forget. Ask Matthews and Brady and Ollinger, or any of the others. Ask Garrett if I forget. Ask him if you could.

Night and day, hear my cry:

I don't forget.

I don't forget.

12

PLUCK FROM THE MEMORY A ROOTED SORROW.

— **SHAKESPEARE**

The sun warm on my shoulders always lulls me to sleep. I was thinking about Tom and Charlie and the others. I was thinking about Manuella in there at her kitchen table with her little glass birds all lined up on the window sill and how she misses Charlie a whole lot more than she will ever miss me. Maybe I was dreaming. Dreams don't stay with me anymore. Sometimes it's hard to know what's a dream and what's not.

A long black automobile drives down the street and the wind it stirs up flaps one of the posters some fellow tacked on the telephone pole. It says Tom Mix will be appearing at the county fair. I'd like to go see him and shake his hand and ask him to show me a rope trick or two. I might even be able to show him a thing or two with those fancy pistols he wears. Big Colts with silver barrels and pearl grips. A two-gun man. Wonder what he'd think if he knew it was *me* showing *him* a thing or two?

Manuella calls my name, asks me to come inside to have lunch with her, but I'm not hungry. These days I'm hardly ever hungry. Least little bit fills me up. She likes soup from a can. All kinds of soup, it doesn't matter which kind. Got a whole cupboard full of canned soup: chicken noodle, vegetable, onion, bean with bacon. Every day she opens one and heats it on the stove, then pours it into a bowl and dips in her bread. Soup, coffee, cigarettes. I don't know what keeps her alive, unless it's the memory of Charlie.

"Henry, come in and eat some soup," she says. I've eaten all the soup I'm going to. Nobody can live on soup. What I'd like is a big beefsteak laid out on a big dinner plate smothered in chilies and frijoles and slopping up those beans with some warm tortillas and a big glass of ice beer to wash it all down with. But hell, I couldn't eat it if I had it. Stomach won't allow it.

I'd like to go and meet Tom Mix, take a ride around the arena on that horse of his, *Tony,* drink a little whiskey with the man. Maybe talk to him a little about the old days.

"Henry, the soup is getting cold."

I try to act like I've nodded off and don't hear.

After a while she stops asking me to come eat with her. I reckon she's got Charlie and those glass birds to keep her company.

We went to Niagara Falls and spent a night in a hotel the same year Teddy Roosevelt came through there and they were popping off fireworks and had electric lights strung in such a way the lights looked like they were down under the water and we could feel the mist from the falls as we stood on the balcony and watched it all. Then she took off her clothes and asked me to take off mine and we stood that way right there on the balcony with the mist falling on our bare skin and the fireworks exploding in the sky and the electric lights down under the water. It was probably the only time she didn't think about Charlie for more than ten minutes. It was like we'd stepped into a different world. Like we'd left one and stepped into another.

I think maybe I'll go down to the county fair and see Tom Mix, see what he can do with those pistolas and his lariat.

"Henry," she says, but I'm already getting up to go.

13

I WONDER BY MY TROTH, WHAT THOU, AND I DID, TILL WE LOVED?

— JOHN DONNE

Isabella and I rode white horses across purple sage — blooded stock all the way from Spain with long sweeping tails and silver-studded saddles. I sang for her by a river and she closed her hands over mine and we danced there with the only music being what was in our hearts.

"Will you stay forever?" she asked and I promised I would.

She undid the strings to her bodice and said, "To seal your promise, Billy, to seal our love," and I took her in my arms and we lay there on the grass a long time, our eyes closed, listening to the water slip its banks, her mouth sweet and tender as a rose petal.

We vowed our love to the lonely sky.

Every wrong thing they ever said about me, this they never knew: Isabella, a fine and prosperous woman, loved me in the tall grass and whispered my name and made me promise that I

would always be hers. A woman of Spanish roy-
alty whose gold could have bought them all, gave
herself to me under a lonely sky.

They say a man traveled the West with a finger
in a jar of brine and charged ten cents to see it,
telling everyone that it was the "trigger finger of
Billy the Kid." Garrett claimed outrage while he
drank his liquor in an El Paso saloon. This thing
had gotten out of hand, this lie of his, and he
knew it. But the lie had sealed his lips and turned
his heart black, and the taste of whiskey bitter as
bile, and this black poison ran through his veins
all the rest of his days.

Isabella and I swam naked and later still slept,
and awoke again and she kissed the puckered
scars the bullets had made in my flesh and where
a knife had once cut me and asked me of my
pain.
"Give me your pain," she said, "and I will
carry it like a small child between my bones."
Her soft words stole my heart forever and
ever.

I understand the love in Manuella's heart for
Charlie, for in my own the self-same ache lin-
gers still. Of love and regret we must never
forget.
Isabella.
Isabella.
Isabella.

Her name like a song given to me at birth so that I can't forget, so that it will go to the grave when I do.

14

MURDER'S OUT OF TUNE,
AND SWEET REVENGE GROWS HARSH.
— SHAKESPEARE

Father stated that someone ran out to pick up either Brady's or Hindman's gun and was shot as he stooped over, not through the bowels, as reported, but through the left thigh. Father said that the man came walking through the door and he treated him by drawing a silk handkerchief through the wound and binding it up. Soon the Murphy-Dolan crowd, who had tracked the man by his blood, came to search the house. It seems that Sam Corbett had taken the wounded man in charge and they disappeared. Afterwards father learned that Sam Corbett had sawed a hole under a bed and laid the man there with a gun in his hand.

— Mrs. Ruth Ealy, daughter of Dr. Ealy

We were regulators, but they called us assassins. Brady's bunch, that is.

Charlie was home with Manuella and Tom was sick with his head in a pail from snakehead whiskey and green apples. But me, McNab, French, Waite, Middleton, and Hendry Brown were fit as fiddles and ready to bring the other side some of their own medicine, which they rightly deserved. We didn't do it, who would?

April first. April Fools'. But the joke's on the other side. I guess it was a perfect day to do some shooting.

Down the street they came under a crimson sky: Brady, Hindman, Matthews, Long, and Peppin, like a clutch of hens heading off to peck. We laid for them behind Tunstall's wall, heavily armed and willing. Maybe it was a mean trick, maybe it wasn't. Maybe it was just tit for tat, giving them what they gave us: bitter medicine. Tunstall sleeps forever.

An eye for an eye, isn't that what the Bible says? You tell me what's wrong with it. Besides, Brady had a rifle of mine I wanted back and I damned well meant to get it. The son of a bitch walked with my gun crooked in his arms. What did he expect? Thief, liar, murdered. He deserved no quarter and we weren't about to give him any. Hendry Brown sniggered as they drew near and said, "Let's shoot their asses off!" and that's what we did.

We opened up as one, the smoke from our guns so thick nobody could see who shot what but we knew we laid into them good. When the smoke cloud drifted away. Brady lay stone dead and Hindman nearly so, shot through the spine and crying out for water till Ike Stockton brought him some in a tin cup and pressed it to his lips. Hindman took one sip and died, the water trickling down his chin, blood leaking from his nostrils.

Over the wall I went to get my rifle, which lay at Brady's feet. That's when Matthews — hiding in a doorway — hit me with a lucky shot through the leg. It stung like a hot nail. I tossed lead his way but he threw himself through a window and blood drained into my boot. The boys scattered and I headed up to Doc Ealy's for repair on the leg. Peppin called in the soldiers and they all looked for me, but by then I was down under the flooring beneath Corbett's bed, down there with the spiders crawling over me, listening to Peppin and the soldiers stomping all around the house, Peppin tossing angry words around about what he was going to do to me once he laid hands on me. I prayed he would tear up those floorboards and look in, see me lying with those pistols resting on my chest, thumbed and ready to go. "Howdy, George," then pull the triggers and serve him lead for breakfast. But his luck held and he failed to look under the bed and pull up the floorboards.

Sam waited a good long while before letting me out.

I ate dinner that night with him and his wife and children. We ate stewed chicken and I thanked him and offered to give him my rifle, the one I'd gotten back from Brady, but he said he wouldn't take it. I stayed that night, sleeping under Sam's bed and listened to the bedsprings and Sam's snores and felt the spiders crawl over me before leaving in the early dawn on a piebald mare Sam had saddled and left tied up behind Tunstall's. I noticed the empty cartridges behind the wall as I went around back there — they looked like severed brass fingers — and rode away to Fort Sumner.

A fine April morning on a high-stepping horse. What could be better.

15

AND I WILL SHOW YOU SOMETHING
  DIFFERENT FROM EITHER
YOUR SHADOW AT MORNING STRIDING
  BEHIND YOU
OR YOUR SHADOW AT EVENING RISING
  TO MEET YOU;
I WILL SHOW YOU FEAR IN A HANDFUL
  OF DUST.

—T. S. ELIOT

Garrett sent word that he would get me. A note written in his own hand and delivered by a boy named Hector Perez.

Killing Brady and Hindman was a mean trick, Kid. And with it, you've sealed your own fate. Why couldn't you have left when you had the chance? Now I'm sworn to duty, can do nothing more for you. I'll see you hanged and help hold the rope.

Garrett

I could smell whiskey on the paper.

I showed it to Celsa, who stood in the moonlight naked, her hips as brown and smooth as polished stone. She said she could not read so I told her what it said.

"You must run, Billy. You must not let him catch you."

We saw a shooting star and she pressed herself to me, her heart beating through my shirt.

She worried about everything. I asked when her husband would return and she kissed my hands and said, not for several days, that he and his brother had a herd of sheep up in the hills and had to protect them from wolves. I thought that any man who would leave his wife unprotected for the sake of sheep asked for what troubles came his way.

That night we listened to the rain and she said she was sad and burned Garrett's note in the flames of a fire that threw shadows on the ceiling. Years later I saw a photograph of her standing in front of an adobe, her skin wrinkled and dark as wet mud, an old woman standing there with a tin pail in her hands and a child clinging to her skirts. She was very fat. Below the photograph it read: *Celsa Gutierrez, girlfriend of Billy the Kid.*

I had a hard time believing it was her. She looked nothing like the pretty young woman who stood naked in the moonlight that night and worried over my fate.

Garrett sleeps in a bed too short for his long legs and the cat licks his feet.

Manuella coughs in the kitchen from her cigarettes, then moves to the living room to sit and put her legs up, the veins blue and ridged and painful, and closes her eyes for a nap. No doubt she dreams of Charlie and Garrett telling her to buy him a new suit of clothes to be buried in. "Send the bill to me," she told me he said.

Which tells you he knew it was murder. Ten dollars' worth of burying clothes is a cheap price to pay for a guilty conscience.

I see horses in my head, sometimes a hundred or more, all colors, their thudding hooves like the beating heart of the land. A dance of horses.

Charlie plays the fiddle, Tom the mouth harp. Celsa sleeps in my arms, waiting for a sheepherder, while I think of a woman south of the border whose tears were as bitter as alkali when we last parted. Happiness is an elusive thing but sorrow is everlasting.

Manuella's snores flutter from her lips like wounded birds, a spot of soup dots her chin. Her fingers are waxy yellow from so many cigarettes; they look like knobby candles in her lap. She is with Charlie now, I'm sure, back there in those old days, a young girl dancing, riding double on a spirited mount behind him, laughing and showing him her breasts and bare legs as they ride swiftly across the buff-colored hills, the wind stringing through her hair.

"Charlie-o-Charlie," she cries with glee. "Charlie-o-Charlie, won't you marry me."

Last Sunday she asked me to go to church with her and I did and I watched her walk to the front and kneel down and let the priest put the wafer in her mouth while he spoke words I could not understand. When she returned she looked more grim than ever. I never understood such business. The dead rising up, praying to ghosts and all that. I said to her, "If you believe that it's true that the dead can rise up again, then why didn't Charlie? Why didn't Tom or any of the others?"

She looked at me for a long, long time, then said, "They were not without sin."

Tom sleeps peaceful as a baby, his guts full of Garrett's lead. Charlie next to him, same thing. Me in the middle, not as dead as Garrett would like me. At night we can hear the Pecos slipping its banks, trying to get at us, to wash us away and all trace of our existence. All day long the wind calls our names. Blue sky, so peaceful. The flesh falls away, the bones remain for a time, then turn to dust, earth reclaimed.

Sabal said to me once, "Are you sleeping with my wife?"

Of course I could have shot him, killed him as easy as a bug, but I lied and denied everything.

I dream of Garrett more often than I care to and awake with sunlight in my eyes.

98

An old sheep-herder who used to rob banks down in Sonora before he grew too old to sit a horse told me this: "No matter which direction we take, we ride straight into the arms of death."

He had a few teeth left and some memories and those damn sheep. He asked me if I'd ever been scared and I told him no. Then he drew a line in the dirt and said, "You ever been shot and piss blood, you know what fear is."

The old women say: "Babies cry because they know what awaits them."

16

FOR YOU AND I ARE PAST OUR DANCING DAYS.

— SHAKESPEARE

Rain awakes me. Where did it come from? Last I knew the sun was warm upon my face. Drips off the eaves of the house. Drip, drip, drip. Tom Mix jumps through a wide loop of his lariat and earns five hundred dollars for half an hour performance. It would take Tom and Charlie and me a month of running stolen beeves to the Panhandle to clear that much money.

Always wash in rainwater, Mother said. Purest water there is, God's tears. She claimed the rains cured catarrh and, if taken on a regular basis, would increase mental capacities and fortify the blood. I hold my tongue out and let the rain drip onto it. It tastes like metal, cool and wet.

It costs half a buck, according to the posters, to go see Tom Mix perform his rope tricks down at the fairgrounds under a big tent. *No Kodaks*

Allowed! Charlie could throw a rope loop so wide Tom could ride through it on his buckskin filly. Charlie learned roping from the Mexican vaqueros, who were the best people with a rope I ever saw. I wonder if Mr. Mix ever seen a Mexican vaquero throw a rope?

"Draw them pistolas, Mr. Mix, and get to fighting!" I imagine in my mind. Why I do not know, except that it is diversionary and keeps me from noticing the brown spots on the backs of my hands and the knobby wrists an inch below my shirt cuffs and the way my clothes hang on me. What I wouldn't give for fifty years back, knowing what I know now. Frank James and Cole Younger went around the country preaching about the evils of outlawry. Imagine a man whose mother had her hand blown off by the Pinkertons sanctifying and standing up for the law! Old men gone to seed. The damage to them done, the bullets still in their muscle. The light of hope dim in their eyes, their brains soft as mush. Frank died with a pocketful of loose change from the tours he sold of the family farm. A long white beard down to his belt buckle. Cole died with empty pockets and a hatful of regrets.

"Henry, you didn't die out there, did you?"

Manuella is up and about, back in the kitchen now, making herself a fresh pot of coffee to have with her cigarettes. I don't answer. She smokes one after another and coughs and stares at her birds.

101

A police car drives by and I just naturally hold my breath. Sure hate to go to the can now, after all these years. John Wesley Hardin spent twenty-five years in the Texas state penitentiary and came out a lawyer. Went in a crook, came out a crook, but at least the kind they wouldn't hang him for. I guess being in the can wasn't a complete waste of his time, but it would be for me. All that time locked up, then set free, and then he gets shot in the head in an El Paso saloon. Man walked up behind him and shot him five or six times. A man with a grudge, they say. Twenty-five years in the can, then somebody shoots him just like that. That's a long time to wait just to be murdered.

Manuella comes out on the porch and stands there, a cigarette between her yellow fingers, the smoke curling into blue ribbons.

"When did it start raining?"

"A little while ago," I say, but I don't remember exactly.

She sniffs the air.

"I always liked the way the air smells when it rains," she says.

She has a faraway look in her eyes. We could just as well be brother and sister, I think — we've come to that after all these years. Two old people living out what's left of our lives together — her with thoughts of Charlie, me with thoughts of Isabella, both of us longing for something we haven't had in years. Longing for the dead, longing for what could have been, what never was. Takes up most of our day, the longing does. But then, there's not much else when you think about it. You live long enough, you spend the first half living life and the second half trying to live it again in your mind.

I know she's been praying all these years that Charlie would rise up from the dead, just like her Jesus, and come back to her, but he won't. Show me a dead man risen up and I'll believe. Till then, it's a hard thing to swallow.

Garrett sleeps in a bed while the cat licks his feet, his pockets empty of reward money never collected. Five hundred dollars was enough to buy him lock stock and barrel, but he went to his grave a Judas. Another fellow that never rose up again.

Manuella smokes and watches the silver rain and I tell her to let it fall on her tongue.

"Why?" she asks.

I can't explain it, the power of rain.

17

I DO NOT SEE THEM HERE; BUT AFTER
  DEATH
GOD KNOWS I KNOW THE FACES I SHALL
  SEE.
EACH ONE A MURDERED SELF, WITH LOW
  LAST BREATH.

— DANTE ROSSETTI

I left word with Wilcox for Bowdre to meet
me at the forks in the road, two mile from
Sumner, at two o'clock the following day. He
kept his appointment. . . . I promised that if
he, Bowdre, would change his evil life and
forsake his disreputable associates, every effort would be made by good citizens to pro-
cure his release on bail and give him an
opportunity to redeem himself.

Bowdre did not seem to place much faith in
these promises and evidently thought I was
playing a game to get him in my power. He,
however, promised to cease all commerce
with the Kid and his gang. He said he could
not help but feed them when they came to his
ranch, but that he would not harbor them
more than he could help. I told him if he did
not quit them or surrender he would be pretty

sure to get captured or killed, as we were after the gang and would sleep on the trail until we took them in, dead or alive. And thus we parted.

— Pat Garrett, *The Authentic Life of Billy the Kid, the Noted Desperado of the Southwest, Whose Deeds of Daring and Blood Made His Name a Terror in New Mexico, Arizona, & Northern Mexico*

Manuella said Charlie took to sleepwalking — she found him standing in the yard one time, a rifle in his hands, staring at nothing at all. She was afraid to wake him because she heard that if you woke a sleeping man suddenly he would die of fright. She said he stood there a long time in his underdrawers and that rifle, staring into the black night, then eventually he went and lay down in the henhouse and awoke with feathers in his hair.

Tom said, "Charlie, what do you want most in this old life?" while we were in Fort Sumner drinking Beaver Smith's homemade liquor. He made it from cactus roots.

"To stay alive and grow old," Charlie said. "That's what I want most. Children maybe."

Tom laughed and said, "Hell, I sure don't want to live to be an old man with no teeth in my head, do you, Billy?"

Tom was wearing a corduroy jacket with the elbows wore out and checked pants. His cowlick stood up like a rooster tail.

"What do you think, Kid, are we going to live a long life?" Charlie asked me. I think he already knew the answer to that one. He looked as glum as any man I ever knew.

"Let's play monte," Tom said, but Charlie was blue and chose to drink Beaver's homemade liquor from a clay jar and keep to his thoughts.

"I walk in my sleep sometimes now," Charlie said. "Manuella found me sleeping with the chickens last week."

Tom looked at me and blinked.

None of us could know that within the month Garrett would kill us all.

Manuella told me that Charlie wanted to quit the fight but didn't trust Garrett.

" 'They have me trapped,' " she said he said. " 'Garrett will kill me either way I jump.' "

She bought him a black suit and combed his hair with rose water and dusted his face with powder and the backs of his hands where they lay folded across his chest. For two days and nights he lay in the living room of their small hacienda as silent as time with a circle of lighted candles around his coffin while she wept and cursed me and Garrett for having killed him.

"Tell me," I said to her one time years and years later when she brought it up again, "did you find any of my bullets in your husband's corpse?"

She didn't speak to me for nearly a month, then when she did she merely asked if I wanted a bowl of soup. After that we took to sleeping in separate beds and she began talking to Charlie at her kitchen table while staring at her glass birds and drinking her coffee.

We end up with the ones we do, but rarely the ones we want. I think of Isabella as I live in the house of another woman.

I was confident that the gang would be in Fort Sumner that night, and made arrangements to receive them. There was an old hospital building on the eastern boundary of the plaza — the direction from which they would come — the wife of Bowdre occupied a room of the building, and I felt sure they would pay their first visit to her. I took my posse there, placed a guard about the house, and awaited their game.

— Pat Garrett

There was snow on the ground, I remember that. And so cold our breath came out like smoke. We were in a festive mood because we'd heard that Garrett had moved out of Sumner and it was near Christmas and Charlie was anxious to see Manuella again — he had a silver ring for her in his pocket that he'd purchased in Sonora. But as we drew near something haunted

107

my thoughts — Garrett's ghost, as it turned out. I could feel his presence and my blood felt full of ice.

The gang was in full sight approaching. In front rode Foliard and Pickett. I was under the porch and close against the wall, partly hidden by some harness hanging there, Chambers close behind me, and the Mexican behind him. I whispered: "That's them."
— Pat Garrett

Something told me it was a bad hand, what we were riding into. I always had good instinct for trouble. I rode back to check behind us, though Garrett claims I turned heels.

I called "Halt!" Foliard reached for his pistol — Chambers and I both fired; his horse wheeled and ran at least one hundred and fifty yards. Quick as possible, I fired at Pickett.
— Pat Garrett

I heard the shots and knew the hand had gone bad, spurred my pony, and yelled at the boys to flee — "It's a goddamn trap!"

When Foliard's horse ran with him, he was uttering cries of mortal agony, and we were convinced that he had received his death. He, however, wheeled his horse and, as he rode slowly back, he said: "Don't shoot, Garrett, I'm killed." Mason called: "Take your medicine old boy, take your medicine," and was going to Foliard.

— Pat Garrett

I could hear Tom's cries rending that brittle night air as piercing as a coyote's howl, as lonely and troubling. I knew they'd shot him to pieces.

I called to Tom to throw up his hands, that I would give him no chance to kill me. He said he was dying and could not throw up his hands, and begged that we would take him off his horse and let him die as easy as possible. Holding our guns down on him we went up, took his gun out of the scabbard, lifted him down, took off his pistol, which was full-cocked, and found that he was shot through the left side, just below the heart, and his coat was cut across the front by a bullet.

— Pat Garrett

Goddamn you, Garrett. Goddamn you to hell. I don't forget. Remember, I don't forget!

After we laid him down inside, he begged me to kill him, said if I was a friend of his I would put him out of his misery. I told him I was no friend to men of his kind who sought to murder me because I tried to do my duty, and that I did not shoot up my friends as he was shot. Just then Mason entered the room again. He changed his tone at once and cried: "Don't shoot anymore, for God's sake, I'm already killed."

— Pat Garrett

Rudabaugh's horse was shot through and through and made it twelve miles before going down. I pulled Dave up back of me and we rode double the rest of the way, Tom's cries still in my ears. I hear him now, plain as anything, crying out, "I've been killed!"

Tom and me lie on a riverbank and dream of whores and hear the water rippling over stones.

He also asked Mason to tell McKinney to write to his grandmother in Texas and inform her of his death. Once he exclaimed: "O! My God, is it possible I must die?" I said to him, just before he died: "Tom, your time is short." He answered: "The sooner the better: I will be out of pain." He died about three quarters of an hour after he was shot.

— Pat Garrett

Tom sleeps in a grave, but not alone. He's got me and Charlie to keep him company and all the stone angels above our heads.

Pals to the very end.

18

**LOST ANGEL OF A RUIN'D PARADISE!
SHE KNEW NOT 'TWAS HER OWN; AS WITH
  NO STAIN
SHE FADED, LIKE A CLOUD WHICH HAD
  OUTWEPT ITS RAIN.**
          — PERCY BYSSHE SHELLEY

Old Mexico is a land of distant dreams where the land has its beauty and the people have their poverty, but Isabella was both beautiful and rich, I tell you. A woman whose wealth was equaled only by her beauty, whose spirit and love flow in my veins still, whose image is as sharp and preserved as that of the Rio Grande. She made me dream of things I'd never before imagined, and opened my heart to new possibilities. And she caused me to forget Lincoln County and Garrett, the blood spilled there, the red-soaked earth.

"Leave that place, Billy, stay here with me." How many times did she whisper those words to me on warm nights. I wanted to, had meant to do just that, stay there with her forever. Say, to hell with Garrett and Dolan and Murphy and the killing and murdering that was going on. It wasn't for me. The taste of blood can turn rancid, even in the mouth of a sinner.

We listened to Spanish guitars under a black velvet night, the stars falling, *onetwothree,* and I wrote a poem for her that had the words *guitars* and *stars* in it. She hugged me and said she would keep it forever. I felt thrilled down to my toes — a woman like her in love with me.

I wore a suit of fine clothes for the first time and she told me how handsome I looked as we had our photograph taken by a man in Sonora, standing side by side as though we were married.

Why I returned North I'll never know, but she said she would always wait for me and I believed that she would, that she would be there waiting forever for me. But death comes like a thief in the night, the Bible says. What we leave behind we cannot always return to. Say your prayers in case you die in your sleep.

She wanted me to sing for her, so I sang "Silver Threads Among the Gold" and it made her cry and when I asked her if my singing was that bad, she laughed, the tears staining her cheeks, and said no, that she was just completely happy. I was too, and later we took off our clothes and swam in the river and I kissed her, her hair wet and heavy in my hands.

"We could be married," she said.

"Is that what you want?"

She closed her eyes and lifted her face to the sun and I kissed her neck.

Being there in the water with her was like being born, like the earth had given birth to us, and we were emerging from its womb, untouched creatures, given to the sun and sky above. Given to each other: Adam and Eve in the garden. The fruit of life, sweet in our mouths.

Then something passed before the sun and cast a shadow and when I looked up I saw a raven with wings spread black against the light. Its caw rippled through the silence as it glided along like it was on a string held by God's own hand, like a black puppet, a dark angel who shouted warning.

Ravens were always a fright to me. Sombrero Jack was the first one to tell me that they were bad luck.

"A raven suddenly appearing out of nowhere is worse than hearing a hoot owl in the night," he said, his eyes narrow with dread. He told me ravens were devil birds and Indians worshiped them.

"An Injun," he said, "will worship anything he don't understand."

Sombrero Jack would shoot any raven he saw and pluck a tail feather from it and stick it in the band of his hat for good luck and to ward off tragedy. A man in Cortez shot him through the eye in a Colorado whorehouse while he was wearing his lucky raven's feather in his sombrero.

I wasn't given to believe most of what he told me. He's the one that got me in dutch in Silver City, and a mighty bad man to begin with. But when the raven's wings blotted the sun as I stood there in the river with Isabella it gave me a sense that my body was filling up with the darkness.

Maybe Sombrero Jack and Indians knew something I didn't.

Later I asked Charlie and Tom what they knew about ravens.

Tom said, "They are big and ugly and a nuisance. I hate being woken up by them early in the morning."

Charlie said he'd heard they were bad luck, but figured it was a lot of idle talk.

Then Tom's dog stood on its hind legs and danced a jig round and round.

I remember now, that the very evening Garrett murdered Tom I'd heard ravens somewhere in the night when we were still a mile out from Sumner.

"Do you think this is what Eden was like?" Isabella asked as we lay on the grass letting the sun dry us, our fingers entwined. I asked where Eden was, because I didn't know back then. She laughed and explained that it was where God put the first two people he ever created and said it was a garden filled with every delight and providing every need. That God had created the man first, then the first woman — that he had fashioned her from the rib of the man.

I told her I thought that it seemed like we were the only two people on earth. She ran off and found a pomegranate tree and picked me an apple.

I said, "What's this?"

"Temptation," she said.

We both laughed and I split it open.

"This is what we call a Chinese apple," I said, picking out the red seeds on the blade of my knife.

She fed them to me one by one while I fell in love.

Her hair was as black as raven feathers.

Tom called his dog Buster. He'd flip over backward for a biscuit and chase after black birds.

Her death put a forever ache in my side — like a rib broken from me. I don't know. Much of what people have told me of God is mumbo jumbo. But still . . .

19

**HOW OFTEN ARE WE TO DIE BEFORE WE GO QUIET OFF THIS STAGE?
IN EVERY FRIEND WE LOSE A PART OF OURSELVES, AND THE BEST PART.**
— ALEXANDER POPE

There was snow on the ground, it was desperately cold and Brazil's beard was full of icicles.
— Pat Garrett

Garrett and his bunch ran us to ground near Stinking Springs. Horses wore out, everyone was tired and hungry and cold. We made an old shack and holed up in it. Charlie and me and the others. Wind was mournful like a grieving woman coming through the cracks, puffs of snow, no heat. Miserable time.

Finding a dry arroyo, we took its bed and were able to approach pretty close. There were three horses tied to projecting rafters of the house, and, knowing that there were five of the gang, we concluded they had led two

116

horses inside. There was no door; only an opening, where a door had once been.

— Pat Garrett

Charlie sat with his knees bent to his chin, his hands shivering with cold, his eyes full of Manuella and loneliness.

The others were still glum over what had happened to Tom. A man cold and hungry with death on his mind doesn't usually have too much to say. It was like a tomb, that little empty house, the door gone, blown off by the wind or stolen. I tried to remain cheerful, but to tell the truth, I couldn't find much to be cheerful about. Some things were worse than dying and this was one of them.

I had a perfect description of the Kid's dress, especially his hat. I had told all the posse that, should the Kid make his appearance, it was my intention to kill him, and the rest would surrender.

— Pat Garrett

Tom waits for Charlie and me in a lonely grave near the Pecos.

The Kid had sworn that he would never yield himself a prisoner, but would die fighting, with a revolver at each ear, and I knew he would keep his word.

— Pat Garrett

117

I thought of Isabella, the warm border, clean white sheets, dancing in water, a blooded horse. The sweetness of pomegranate seeds. Tender moments.

Charlie said, his teeth chattering, "You don't have no whiskey or tack in your hat, do you, Bill?" I was wearing the same hat I wore when that fellow in Fort Sumner took a tintype photograph of me just in off the Llano the winter before — the "famous" tintype. Only my poor hat was a lot more busted and stove in now. Bought it in Las Vegas that time I went up there and drank tequila with Frank and Jesse James. They wanted to rob New Mexican banks and I just laughed and said, you boys better keep to Missouri where the law isn't so deadly. These stars down here would just as soon shoot you as look at you. Jess had those clear eyes and handsome looks and I knew there wasn't a thing that worried him — not even New Mexican peace officers.

Charlie said, "Damn if I don't have to piss. Can I borry your hat, Bill, so my ears don't freeze off?"

"Your doodle might," I said, and he let his mouth twist crooked while he stuffed my plug hat down over his ears.

"Manuella would run me off if I was so careless as to let my doodle freeze off" was the last cheerful words I heard him say.

He grabbed up a feedbag of grain on his way out. Charlie was always particular about caring for his animals. The rancher in him.

Before it was fairly daylight, a man appeared at the entrance with a nose bag in his hand, whom I firmly believed to be the Kid. His size and dress, especially the hat, corresponded with his description exactly. I gave the signal by bringing my gun to my shoulder, my men raised, and seven bullets sped on their errand of death. Our victim was Charley Bowdre.
— Pat Garrett

It sounded like wood splintering, then Charlie cried out the same as Tom had, that same death keen. He staggered backward through the door, still holding the feedbag, blood dripping into the grain, leaking through his fingers.

"I'm killed, Bill. Garrett's gone and killed me the same way he murdered Tom. *Christ almighty,* look at me!"

The Kid caught hold of his belt, drew his revolver around in front of him, and said: "They have murdered you, Charley, but you can get revenge. Kill some of the sons a bitches before you die."
— Pat Garrett

That part is true. Maybe the only true thing Garrett ever said about me in that whole book he wrote about me.

Bowdre came out, his pistol still hanging in front of him, but with his hands up. He walked toward our ranks until he recognized me, then came straight to me, motioned with his hand toward the house, and strangling with blood, said: "I wish — I wish — I wish —" then, in a whimper: "I'm dying!" I took hold of him, laid him gently on my blankets, and he died almost immediately.

— Pat Garrett

Garrett called for us to surrender, but I was ready to ride out into them, killing all I could before they killed me. I had my racer inside the house and Charlie's was there too. Wilson said, "What are we going to do, Kid?" I told him I was going to ride out and kill as many as I could and if he was any sort of a badman he'd do the same — that maybe, with luck, we could ride right through them. Then Garrett did a mean thing and shot one of the horses outside so that it fell into the door blocking the way. Wilson, Pickett, and Rudabaugh voted that we surrender. I said, fine, if that's what you girls want then let's get it over with and we did. I knew Garrett wouldn't hold me for long, so I went along with it. A belly full of beans is better than one full of lead.

The whole ride back to Sumner all I thought about was a raven, its wings spread black against the sun, and the weight of Isabella's wet hair in my hands.

Manuella said just this when Garrett gave her Charlie's body: "Oh, no!"

Tom says, "Welcome, Charlie, I was getting mighty lonesome here with naught but the Pecos to whisper in my ears. Where's Billy?"

"He'll be along soon," Charlie says. "Garrett's going to send him."

"That long-legged son of a bitch just won't quit, will he?"

"No. He won't quit. Not till we're all three laid here to rest."

"Pals," says Tom.

"Pals," Charlie says.

Pals.

20

THE ACCUSING SPIRIT, WHICH FLEW UP TO
HEAVEN'S CHANCERY WITH THE OATH,
BLUSHED AS HE GAVE IT IN; AND THE
RECORDING ANGEL, AS HE WROTE IT
DOWN, DROPPED A TEAR UPON THE WORD
AND BLOTTED IT OUT FOR EVER.
— LAURENCE STERNE

Manuella sits under the glow of an electric
light, her fingers busy with knitting needles
and cigarettes — who she knits for, I don't
know. A sweater, her third this year, this one
navy blue like the others. I think that someday
she will knit one for me, say, here, Henry, this
is to keep those old bones of yours warm, since
I can't do it myself. But she never does. Just
knits them, then puts them away somewhere
like she's saving them for somebody. Charlie
maybe.

I watch her knit and want to take a walk down
to the tavern — have me a shot of tequila, the old
kind we used to drink, Tom, Charlie, and me.
The kind with the worm down in the bottom of

the bottle that we could crunch between our teeth. Once, on the Llano, Tom shot a nigger soldier in the hand because he ate the worm. Tom was crazy when he was on tequila.

"Who are you knitting those sweaters for?" I say, for no good reason other than I'm bored as hell waiting for something to happen because I never could stand just sitting around without a plan.

Manuella looks up at me. She refuses to wear spectacles so her eyes looked pinched. She takes a draw from her cigarette and looks at me like I'm some sort of a monkey in the circus, then blows out a ring of smoke.

"Why do they have to be for someone?" she says.

"What good is a sweater nobody wears?"

"*Ahhh*, Henry," she says and goes back to what she's doing.

I leave her like that and go to my bedroom, where there is a small desk, and take out my journal; it seems the only thing that keeps me breathing. I'm writing everything down because someday I want the truth to come out, what Garrett did and what I did and did not do. I want to tell about Isabella and Celsa and Charlie and Tom. John Tunstall. All the others, Susan McSween, John Chisum, and Sallie — all of them. I want to tell my side of it. Goddamn, is there anything wrong with that?

There, right there on the first page, read what it says.

123

I killed men, plenty, but only because they tried killing me.

The very first words I ever put down. Truth starts and ends in the same place. I believe that.

Then underneath that first entry, you can see what I wrote:

I never wanted to kill anybody, but sometimes this old life don't give you a choice.

I was still young when I wrote those words. Now I put more thought into everything because I want to get it right, say it right. I started writing this after Charlie and Tom were murdered. After the death of Isabella. *Poor* Isabella. I wrote it all in my head, then put it in this journal because I had to keep it somewhere but in my head.

I can't hardly write some days because my eyes water up thinking about Isabella. Sometimes I am full of her presence. She is at my door or in this room or in the bed next to me. Sometimes out there on the porch sitting with me while I watch automobiles go up and down the street and a man tacks Tom Mix posters on the telephone pole.

Would that death preserve her in a way that life could not. I think I read that somewhere and am going to put it in the journal.

The way I understood it happened was, some vaqueros stole infected blankets from a small band of Apaches, whose bodies they found at the edge of an arroyo. And not understanding that there was death in those blankets, they brought them back to Isabella as gifts, thinking they were doing her a favor. Shortly after she fell ill, and shortly after that died, her flesh scored by the pox. Beside her bed she had the photograph taken of me and her in Sonora. I was told this by a horse-breaker who worked on the ranchero. He said her family buried the tin-type with her, placed it in the lid of her coffin so that she could always look at it on her endless journey.

The Mexes celebrate death but I do not. They have a holiday to honor the dead. But if they knew her the way I knew her they would mourn, not celebrate.

In the right-hand drawer are letters she wrote to me, bundled together by a bright red ribbon.

In the left-hand drawer is a Colt's Lightning .44 with ivory grips. It has shed blood, but none that didn't need it. Maybe when the time is right, it will shed my own.

But not now. Not just yet.

I must write of Isabella now, of the smoothness of her skin against my cheek, of her eyes that always seemed so full of wonder, as if she were seeing everything for the first time, of her hands whose warmth took away my coldness.

I must write to remember.

I must write to forget.

Garrett rides a ghost-white horse across the midnight sky.

Pieces of him fall like broken stars.

Mother said, "Hold out your tongue and taste the rain."

Joe died in a hotel room in Denver, alone, his blood full of whiskey, another life wasted.

My pen begins to scratch at the rough paper.

Dear Isabella, I haven't forgotten you . . . I don't forget. . . .

21

WHY, MAN, HE DOTH BESTRIDE THE
  NARROW WORLD
LIKE A COLOSSUS; AND WE PETTY MEN
WALK UNDER HIS HUGE LEGS, AND PEEP
  ABOUT
TO FIND OURSELVES DISHONORABLE
  GRAVES.
MEN AT SOME TIME ARE MASTERS OF
  THEIR FATES:
THE FAULT, DEAR BRUTUS, IS NOT IN
  OUR STARS,
BUT IN OURSELVES, THAT WE ARE
  UNDERLINGS.
                      — SHAKESPEARE

Garrett said, "Kid, you've killed your last man"
— me shackled to a wagon on a long cold trip to
Santa Fe. "I will take you there for your hanging.
You've lived a very wasted life."

"Don't preach, Pat, it doesn't suit you," I told
him.

"No one will mourn you, Billy. No one will
miss your presence."

"Maybe not, but if you listen carefully when the stars are out you might just hear a senorita or two singing my name."

"You've run out your string, Kid. Your days of whoring and monte are through. John Chisum will sleep well tonight knowing you'll steal no more of his beeves."

"Don't spring the trap just yet, boyo, you don't have the rope around my neck yet."

"Your pals are all dead, Kid. I killed Tom and I killed Charlie and if you hadn't given up back there I would have killed you too. That's been my aim all along."

"I know, darling Pat. I knew it in that whorehouse in Sonora that night you tried to stick it in that fat senorita and broke the bed — back when you were just a long-legged son of a bitch trying to figure where your next meal was coming from."

"You should have killed me when you were thinking about it, Kid. Now it's too late."

"You are right, I should have killed you," I said, then Dave Rudabaugh farted on the seat next to me and laughed.

"I knew a woman in Texas who believed the devil came to her room every night until he got her knocked up," Dave said, after Pat got indignant and rode on ahead of the wagon. "She was a pretty yellow-headed gal with different color eyes. One was blue and one was brown. Crazy as a goddamn loon."

"Maybe that's why the devil screwed her," I said, "because she had different colored eyes."

Dave laughed and farted again and said, "I ate too many of Pat's beans."

Billy Wilson, a pal and a counterfeiter, had his head hung low, his wrists and ankles shackled just like Dave and me. He'd lost his hat somewhere and his hair fluttered like dirty brown ribbons in the bitter wind.

He'd lost heart.

Christmas Day and look where I am, chained in the back of a wagon like a dog.

The most important arrivals on the last night's train were Billy the Kid, Rudabaugh, and Billie Wilson, whom it is unnecessary to introduce to the readers of the *New Mexican*. Everybody in the territory has probably heard of the famous outlaws who have so long infested the country and filled the papers with accounts of crime; and every law-abiding man will be delighted to hear that they were safely landed in the Santa Fe jail. For this great boon Sheriff Pat Garrett and his posse of brave men are to be thanked.

— *Santa Fe New Mexican*,
December 28, 1880

Santa Fe had lost its charm that particular night. Billy Wilson wept in the shadows while Dave and me made plans to bust out. We started digging a hole in the wall with our soup spoons and filling one of the mattresses with the loose dirt and stones.

129

Hell, we were nearly dug through when a deputy showed up and showed his shotgun through the bars. Those hammers clicking back put an end to our mining career.

Dave farted and said, "Oh, well, you can't blame a feller for trying."

I asked for a pencil and some paper and sat down and wrote Governor Wallace a note asking him to come see me, to keep his earlier promises of amnesty that he'd made me personally. I had the papers he'd written me and was willing to show them publicly to the newspapers if he didn't come and keep his promises. I figured if there was a half-honest, half-decent man among the bunch it would be Wallace. He proved me wrong.

> I knew what the papers were, and I proceeded to forestall any move on his part by giving them to the newspapers myself with an account of just how I'd come to make the promises contained therein. When this material appeared in print, I sent a copy to the Kid. I heard nothing further from him, and I presume he understood that the door of my clemency was shut.
>
> — Lew Wallace, Territorial Governor

> . . . Oftentimes, to win us to our harm.
> The instruments of darkness tell us truths,
> Win us with honest trifles, to betray 's
> In deepest consequence.

William Shakespeare wrote that in one of his plays, *Macbeth*, I believe, and I think he had it right, along with a lot of other things he wrote. I keep a copy of his works atop my desk, where I keep the journal, and over the last years of my long life have come to understand more about who we were back then: Garrett, Wallace, Tom, Charlie, and me. If I'd known then what I know now things might have turned out differently. But our youth is all we have when we are young and do with it the best we know how and suffer the consequences of our acts.

Those days in that cold jail got me to thinking.
Would it be death, or life?
I was twenty going on a hundred.

22

**BUT THESE ARE THE DEEDS WHICH SHOULD
NOT PASS AWAY,
AND NAMES THAT MUST NOT WITHER.**
— LORD BYRON

I read that fellow over in Hico, Texas, died yesterday; there is an article in the paper about it. Called himself "Brushy" Bill Roberts, claimed he was me, but fell apart under the questions which should have proved he wasn't me. I know who he was. He was down in that territory all right. I knew him pretty good too. But I'm not saying who he was because he lied and was playing off my name. Any man who won't own up to who he is, what his sins are, don't deserve recognition. Who'd he think was going to believe him? I think if Jesus Christ himself were to come back to earth this afternoon there wouldn't be a handful of people who would believe him. So why should anybody believe a fake like Roberts?

Celsa used to read me the Bible when I'd come down from the hills and Sabal was off with his sheep and after we'd screw. Maybe she read me the Bible out of guilt or something.

We got into it once over whether Jesus was a white man or a Mexican. She thought he was a Mexican. I had to laugh at that. I said, you ever hear of a Mexican could walk on water?

She said I had too much gringo in me sometimes. I probably did and still do.

I don't get how they can kill a fellow and him come back to life later, I said. I figured if we were going to get into it, we might as well get into it good. A lot of it just didn't make any sense to me back then. A lot of it still don't.

Years later, after Sabal left her and she was living near Las Cruces, I dropped in and paid her a visit.

"I thought Garrett killed you," she said. She acted very surprised to see me. She was probably around thirty or forty years old by then.

"Course not," I told her. "Garrett couldn't kill me in his dreams."

"You understand now," she said.

"Understand what?"

"How a man can die and come back to life."

I guess she had me there.

"I used to go and put flowers on your grave," she said. "Sabal would beat me because he said that it was one thing for me to embarrass him when you were alive, but that he wouldn't accept my loving a dead man. He called me a puta and would force himself on me as though that would do it — would stop my desire for you."

"Whatever happened to him?" I said, for by

then I was no longer in love with her but still considered myself her friend.

"He got drunk and went off one day to tend his sheep and didn't come back."

I sat at her table and drank coffee.

"I guess he either got lost or he just forgot to stop walking," she said.

"Which way was he going when you saw him last?" I asked.

"North."

"Then maybe he walked all the way to Canada," I said.

"How far is that?" she said.

"Pretty far, that's all I know."

That seemed to satisfy whatever curiosity she had about it.

"Maybe someday he will come back, show up at your door like I did," I said.

"Maybe, but I don't care about him anymore," she said. "Once a man leaves you and doesn't come back for a long time, you find out you don't need him as much as you thought you did. In fact, if he is still alive, I hope he doesn't come back here looking for me. Let him stay up there in Canada." She looked at me for a long time without taking her eyes away. It made me restless to be there, sitting there at her table drinking coffee with her and talking about her husband.

"I see you have grown a beard and moustaches," she said after a time of not saying anything.

"Yes," I told her. "But mostly I did it so

people won't recognize me when I come back to the territory; I think there is still a reward out for me in some places."

"All that hair on your face makes you look like a hombre," she said, "someone very dangerous."

"Si, a very bad hombre."

"And you've put on some weight too," she said. "You always used to be so skinny."

"Yes," I said, and pushed out my belly until she laughed.

"You know, my sister told me that Garrett never sleeps at night, that he gets up four or five times during the night and just walks around the room and looks out the windows, especially when the moon is full."

"The moon was full the night he shot Billy Barlow," I said. "He knows what he did. You know the Bible says that death comes like a thief in the night. Maybe that's what Pat is worried about, that death will come like a thief in the night and snatch him up."

"Maybe," she said. "Paulina said that they might go to Texas, that he's trying to find some decent work down there."

"Nothing good is ever going to happen for Garrett," I said. "A man always has to pay for his sins, that's what the Bible says."

"You sound like a priest," she said.

"We're all God's doing — the good and the bad of us. Whatever we are, it's because God himself made us that way. He made Garrett and he made Charlie and Tom and me. You tell me which of us is better, which is worse, if we're all made the same, if we all came from the same mud."

"I get headaches," she said suddenly. "Sometimes for days. I have to stay in bed with a cold cloth over my eyes and try not to move. I have some medicine the doctor gave me."

"You getting a headache now?" I asked, and she said she was, so we left it at that and I never saw her again except for that photograph of her in a book when she was an old woman standing in front of an adobe with a tin pail in her hands and below it, it said: *Celsa Gutierrez, girlfriend of Billy the Kid.*

Funny, sometimes it seems as though none of it ever happened. Like as though Celsa never existed except in my mind. Like none of the others did either. Like I didn't . . . that it wasn't me whose life I keep looking back on but someone else's.

I look at the names I've written in my book, but they don't mean anything — just names. Just curls of ink dried black.

Celsa
Tom
Charlie
Isabella
Susan McSween
Sallie Chisum
Ol' John

All the others.

23

**KINGLY CONCLAVES STERN AND COLD
WHERE BLOOD WITH GUILT IS BOUGHT AND
SOLD.**

— PERCY BYSSHE SHELLEY

They tried me twice for murder in one day —
now that's a record of some sorts, I'd imagine.

The building is still there on the corner in the
town square of Mesilla, where I used to drink
and play a little monte and faro. In the plaza
we'd dance under a silver moon and the musicians would have tiny bells sewn to their trouser
legs. Mesilla's where Tom fell in love with a
harelipped gal and swore he'd marry her. He put
a seed in her and when her daddy found out he
shipped her off to a convent down in Sonora.
Tom stayed glum for several days and he
received a letter from her one time saying the
baby had been born with blue eyes and was
beautiful and fat.

He said, "Billy, I have a fat son with my eyes."
Charlie teased him and said, "If he's got your
eyes, how you going to see?"

We were all the time trying to make the other the butt of our jokes. Tom got even a few days later by giving Charlie a hot foot while he was taking a siesta. Charlie yelped like a scalded dog and stomped his hot foot in a horse trough and got his boot full of water.

You go down to Mesilla these days the court is a store that sells dry beans and canned meat, and Garrett and Bristol, the judge who tried me, are *dead, dead, dead.* So are most of the others. Manuella and me have outlived them all. I've been shot, stabbed, hanged, and burned, but I'm still here. You can't kill me is what I kept telling Garrett.

Bristol leaned over his bench and asked: "You got a lawyer, Billy?"

"Un-huh."

"Can you afford a lawyer?"

"Un-huh."

"Then I appoint for your defense, lawyer Fountain. Albert, hie up here and put up a defense for this boy," and a fellow with thick spectacles came forth and stood beside me and hawked and spit and said, "Yes, sir."

So that's how it went.

First trial was for Bernstein, the agency clerk over on the Mescalero Apache reservation they claimed I murdered. Course, they hadn't anything to go by, so the jury didn't even leave the box but sat right there and said, "Not guilty" — and I wasn't, at least in my eyes I wasn't.

But hell, they were just getting warmed up.

Dad Peppin, Billy Matthews, and Baca all testified they'd seen me shoot Brady. How they could have seen it, I don't know — wasn't a one of them behind that wall that day. Fountain argued up one side and down the other about my innocence, about the gunsmoke being so thick nobody could see who was shooting who, and so many shots having been fired that nobody could trace which bullet came from which gun. But they needed to hang someone for Brady and since I was the only one left, guess who they decided to hang?

Then Bristol wanted to know if I had anything to say on my behalf.

"Murder is murder," I said, "no matter how you cut it, judge. You say I murdered Brady and now you are going to murder me. You tell me what the difference is. 'Truth will come to light; murder will not be long hid.' "

The old boy blinked and said, "That's fancy talk for a ruffian killer, Kid."

"A fellow named Shakespeare said it first," I said. He asked how an ignorant boy like myself came by such knowledge and I told him Tunstall gave me some of his books to read — this was before ol' Billy Matthews, one of my accusers, murdered him (I made sure to mention that fact) — "and introduced me to higher thoughts." Judge Bristol hawked and cleared his throat and said, "Have you got anything else to say?" I told him, "Just one thing."

"Well, go on and say it then."

"I don't forget," I said. "I don't ever forget."

Here I was chained up like a dog, wrist to ankle, but you'd never know it by my bravado.

It took some of the bark off the old boy but not enough, for he passed sentence on me and dropped the gavel, and next I knew, Ollinger — himself a cold murderer — was taking me to Lincoln to sit in jail until the hanging day. May thirteenth was what Bristol declared. I was to hang in the spring when wildflowers — lupine and Indian paintbrush — bloom, when the red fruit of the prickly pear begins to ripen. Celsa used to make a jam from those prickly pear and once I rubbed some on her breasts and licked it off. She said Sabal would never think of doing such a thing and laughed.

That evening, while waiting to leave first thing in the morning with Ollinger and Woods, I watched sweethearts dance in the plaza under a silver moon and wished I was among them, a senorita in each arm, my mouth wanting to be sweet with prickly pear jam.

"I guess your last dance will be at the end of a rope, Kid," Ollinger said. "Unless you don't make it to Lincoln alive."

"It might be you who don't make it to Lincoln alive, Bob," I said.

He drew his pistol and threatened to shoot me then and there, but knew if he did he couldn't lie his way out like he did with the others he'd murdered: Bob Jones, Juan Chavez, John Hill.

"How you going to lie your way out of it this time, Bob, shooting a man locked up in the can? You got the pistol, all you have to do is pull the trigger and trade places with me on that gallows. Maybe it's you who will do the dancing at the end of a rope."

He was a big, vain son of a bitch and I knew one of us wouldn't be much longer for this world.

After I killed him I rode to Celsa's and we lay in the dark and listened to the far-off sound of her husband's sheep, and she asked me why I was so hungry for her that night. I didn't know how to explain it because I didn't know myself why I was.

"Pull that fucking trigger, Bob, or quit pointing your pistola at me."

All the rest of that night I listened to the music of the guitars and the laughter of the dancing sweethearts.

Tom and Charlie sleep near a brown snake of a river called the Pecos.

I awaken to church bells and the sound of rain.

I am dancing in the light.

And the light becomes who I am, who I will always be.

24

O SORROW, WILT THOU LIVE WITH ME
NO CASUAL MISTRESS, BUT A WIFE.
     — ALFRED, LORD TENNYSON

"Henry?"

I open my eyes.

"I'd like to go for a walk."

It's close to evening, cicadas buzz in the acacia trees.

"It's such a nice night, I thought we could walk down to that little park where the children play." Manuella has her shawl draped over her shoulders.

Look at us, two old people walking in the twilight, harmless as June bugs. You'd never know the life we lived, the men I shot, the tears she's wept, the rivers of blood, the empty beds.

The air is warm and sweet with honey mesquite, the sky is black silver. Stars flung across the heavens and time is passing more quickly than I care to think about.

"We could stop for an ice cream," she says. There's a store not far from the park that sells twenty flavors of ice cream.

I walk along with my thoughts, she with hers.

A youngster comes by on a blue bicycle, falls, skins his knee, yelps, rights himself, and hurries off.

"Charlie had a bicycle once," Manuella says.

"I never knew that."

"There's lots about Charlie you didn't know," she says.

"What happened to it, his bicycle?"

She shrugs and the knobs of her shoulders poke up against the thin fabric of her dress, the shawl. She is all bird bones.

"I don't remember."

I think about this as we walk, Charlie owning a bicycle, and why he never mentioned it to me.

"How come I never saw him ride it?" I ask. More and more I concern myself with the small things of life because all the big things have become too great to contemplate.

"One of the tires went flat and he never got around to fixing it," she says. "I remember seeing it in the chicken coop. But I don't remember whatever happened to it."

"Maybe he was hoping those chickens would learn how to ride," I say. "That way they could ride up to the house and deliver their eggs fresh."

She looks at me out of the corner of her eye, her lips twisting slightly like she wants to laugh at my foolishness. But she holds too much against me to laugh at anything I say.

"You don't think that's funny, huh?"

"You know how I feel about you and your ways," she says.

We arrive at the park and I say, "Let's sit on that bench for a minute or two." I don't want to admit it but the walk has winded me.

After we're sitting I say, "Why'd you ever take up with me if you hate me so much?"

She nibbles at her lower lip like it's worrisome to her.

"I didn't hate you until Garrett brought Charlie to me," she says.

"I didn't kill Charlie. Garrett killed him."

"He was *with* you, Henry. He should have been home with me."

"It was his choice."

"No," she says. "He was like your hound dog. Everywhere you went, he wanted to go too. I wasn't enough for him once he got a whiff of you."

"Charlie had fire in his blood," I say. "I didn't put it there."

"He was my *goddamn* husband, Henry. He had no right to be off with you."

It's the first time I've ever heard her curse. Even with Charlie lying in her arms, cold and his face like gray ash, she never cursed aloud.

Children ride a merry-go-round in the twilight, their mamas watching and sometimes giving an extra push. The North Star winks like an eye.

"I still don't see why if you hated me you agreed to go away with me," I say.

The children are shrill, their laughter sharp and thin as their slender bodies.

She turns her eyes away and stares at the squealing children. I know what's she thinking.

"I thought if I went with you," she says in a tired way, "that I would be there when you died, Henry. That I would be the one to throw the first clod of dirt on your coffin and in that way I would be able to pay you back a little for Charlie."

The mothers call to the children, telling them it is time they went home. The children protest and elicit one more go-round. Then they all tramp off into the growing darkness and I can hear only the air that she breathes through her smoke-parched nostrils as it bellows into her weak lungs.

"Well, that's a damn poor way to show your gratitude," I say. I confess inwardly that my thoughts are aimless, my argument weak, my bitterness hardly more than a drunk's punch into thin air.

She remains as silent and still as the abandoned merry-go-round.

"What about that time at Niagara Falls?" I say. "Were you wishing me dead there on the balcony with all your clothes off? Did you wish I was dead and unable to take you? Are you telling me that you were doing it just so you can be there when I die, just so you can be the one throws dirt on me?"

"I taught myself to forget at times, Henry,"

she says. "I had to learn to forget or I might have killed you. Or killed me."

"Why don't I walk on back to the house and get my pistol and bring it to you, then you won't have to wait one more minute. You can see it finished here and now, have a direct hand in it. Goddamn if I ain't ready, Manuella. I've lived about all this life I can stand." I start to get up and walk back to the house to get my pistol. Dying would be like a sweet victory after all this time. She'd be doing me a favor.

She takes my hand and grips it tightly and weeps.

I wait for some of her bitter sorrow to pass, then say, "Come'n, I'll buy you an ice cream in a sugar cone."

The spell broken, at least for now, she wipes her eyes and tells me she did not mean to say that she wanted to be the first to throw the dirt o'er me.

Why not her?

Anyone has the right, she has.

I was born of woman and am willing to die at the hands of one.

All the sorrow in the world cannot save us.

All the prayer.

All the love.

We come to the end knowing what we know. Truth strangles the life from us, squeezes and squeezes until we are finished. And we die with the truth still in our throats like bad meat.

146

A bullet would be preferable to waiting.

We eat ice cream in the gloaming, like children tired from play, our lips cold, our tongues licking away.

Old children are what we've become.

From cradle to grave they say, but what is a grave but an earthen cradle to hold our bones till the heavens or hell claims us.

25

THAT SWEET BONDAGE WHICH
IS FREEDOM'S SELF.
— PERCY BYSSHE SHELLEY

Bell and Ollinger sat and stared at me like dogs slavering over a meat bone.

Ollinger told Bell to make sure to keep me chained to the ring bolted in the floor.

"Ain't it enough he's shackled like a nigger?" Bell said.

"You keep that little sumbitch chained up or he'll bite you," Ollinger said, his big belly hanging over his belt buckle like a sack of corn. "Was me, I'd shoot his goddamn face off!"

Bell was not a bad sort. His eyes slanted down like a Chinaman's and he had a black sore on his lip.

"Welcome to the Hotel Murphy," he said, trying to put a lighter touch on it. Ollinger hawked and spit into a can between his boots, a shotgun laid across his knees.

I looked out one of the east windows and saw Tunstall's store, McSween's burned-out house, the brown hills dotted with juniper. Saw the Rio Bonito glittering beyond the cottonwoods running free. A part of me felt like that river.

Least I could see something besides the hangdog faces of my death watch staring back at me.

"Bust out that checkerboard, J.W., and let's have us a game," I said to Bell.

Ollinger hawked and spit again and hitched up his pants as he stood.

"I'm going over to the Wortely for some grub," he declared. "You keep that mean little peckerwood chained up, you hear me?"

Bell nodded his head and shifted his pipe away from the black sore. Soon as Ollinger was down the stairs and crossing the street, Bell broke out the checkerboard and said, "You any good, Kid?"

"Me and my brother Joe used to play till the cows came home," I said. "I can whip the ass off a fat man when it comes to checkers."

"Never knew you had a brother, Kid."

I thought of Joe, off somewhere by his lonesome doing who knew what, me chained to a floor. Hated to have him see me like this. Hated for anybody who knew me to see me like this.

"You ever drink rainwater?" I said to Bell, thinking of what Mother told me about its qualities — how she'd have shed a barrel of tears if she saw her boy chained to the floor like a dog.

He'd taken the black, me the red, and said, "You go first, Kid, fire before smoke," so I did and had him whipped in a dozen moves.

"Rainwater?" he said, like the words finally got through to his brains.

"It purifies the blood," I said.

"God's tears," said Bell, "that's what rain is."

"That's the same thing my mama used to say. You think the almighty weeps for us, J.W.?"

"Maybe not us in particular, Kid, but for us in general."

"You think Jesus was a Mexican?" I asked.

Bell nubbed back his sombrero (didn't he know it was bad luck to wear your hat indoors?) and grinned, the black sore like a raisin on his bloodless lips.

"Mexican? Whatever gave you the idea Jesus was a Mexican?" he said.

"Just something a woman I know believes."

Bell grinned like a monkey that just saw himself in a mirror.

"Hell, Kid, women are peculiar creatures, but I never heard nothing about Jesus being a Mexican. You think maybe he was?"

"Why not?"

"Might as well say he was a nigger as to say he was a Mexican," Bell said, setting up the board for another game. "Or a goddamn Chinaman for that matter."

Bell was wearing a single-action Colt revolver in his belt and every time he moved it winked at me like a senorita wanting to dance.

"Bell, I could play better if you'd unshackle me and let me squat atop the table."

He looked at the chain running from my leg irons down to the ring bolted in the floor.

"You play good enough," he said.

"You can hook me up again when you hear Bob coming up the stairs if that's what you're worried about," I said.

He twisted his mouth.

"You know if you try anything I'll be forced to shoot you, Billy, chained up or no. I'd hate like hell to shoot a chained man, but goddamn if I won't."

"I know you would, J.W., but hell, if I wanted to commit suicide I'd done it before now."

He unhooked me from the ring.

"I'd like to shuffle over to the window and look out before we start a new game. That all right with you?"

"Sure, Kid, just don't try jumping or I'll have to shoot you like a bird on the wing."

I saw Dolan standing on the street, a woman next to him holding a green parasol, two or three other men with them. He must have sensed it because he looked up and saw me watching him, then turned away and walked off with the woman and the other men, their shadows long on the street.

The wind shifted just right and I could smell the river. Then a crow settled onto the branch of a box elder behind McSween's and I remembered what Sombrero Jack told me about crows and knew somebody was in for some bad luck soon.

Later that afternoon Mrs. Lensett, a local woman whose children I'd ridden on my gray pony, came to see me and brought a tin full of sorghum cookies, which Ollinger wouldn't let me have. She had gray speckled eyes and brown ringlets that sprang from her bonnet.

"Are they really going to hang you, Billy?" she said.

"I'd have to be here for them to do that," I said.

She looked at Bob, who never took his eyes off us.

Bob belched and said, "You are invited to see the Kid dance. Make sure to bring your youngsters so they can see what happens to lawbreakers."

I asked her if she would mail a letter for me but Bob wouldn't hear of it and finally she left and I listened to her footsteps all the way down the stairs. Bob ate some of the cookies and threw the rest out the window, then sat and stared at me while he thumbed and released the hammers on his shotgun — *click, click, click,* like false teeth rattling in the head of a dead man, which is what he was only he didn't know it yet.

That night I listened to Bell's snores as he slept sitting in a chair and stared up at the far-flung stars where Tom and Charlie were riding wild ponies and dancing on the moon. A hoot owl called my name and I feel myself sprout wings.

The river runs even in the dark.

26

**A LONELY IMPULSE OF DELIGHT
DROVE TO THIS TUMULT IN THE CLOUDS.
— W. B. YEATS**

I'd gone to Texas. Used some of the money that Susan McSween had given me and went to Texas. Goddamndest thing, fate is. Had no idea what I was going to do except clear out of New Mexico until I could arrange things and settle scores. And I had plenty of scores to settle.

Paid a visit to Tom's folks in Uvalde. Figured someone should tell them the news.

I asked around and got directions to a little white clapboard house near the center of town. There were two blue hogs in the front yard rooting in a trough and they stopped and stared at me and grunted when I walked up.

"Git, you hogs!"

A man was sitting on a tin pail trimming his toenails with a Barlow knife. He had a big head and big feet but the rest of him was as spare as a slab of bacon. I asked if his name was O'Folliard and saw him wince.

153

"You come about my boy?" he said. "If so, he ain't here."

"No, sir," I said. "I've not come looking for him."

"Then what?" he said.

"I've come to tell you Tom is dead."

He stopped paring the nail on his big toe, then let his whole foot flop off his knee and slap the ground.

"I figured sooner or later someone would come and tell me Tom's been murdered. How'd it happen?"

"Lawman shot him in the guts," I said.

The man closed his eyes and tilted his head back until the apple in his neck bobbed like he was trying to drink the news down.

"Lord *God*," he muttered.

Then he opened his eyes and looked at me.

"Were you there when it happened?"

"Yes, sir."

He looked me over good then and said, "I wish you had brought better news. I better go tell the old woman so she'll know."

I waited while he went inside the house and watched the blue hogs jostling each other and rolling around in the mud hole they'd created. They finally came to a blissful rest like two fat children tired from play.

The door to the house swung open and a young, butter-haired woman stood there staring at me. She was tall and thin and had the same bright blue eyes and long face as Tom's.

"Were you Tom's friend?" she said.

"Yes, I was his good pal," I told her.

"I'm Fannie," she said. "Tom's sister."

"I never knew Tom had a sister," I said. "He never mentioned it."

She looked over her shoulder, through the open door of the house. I could hear the old man talking to someone.

"I wish you would have brought him home with you," Fannie said.

I thought of that long ride and what it would do to a body, all those days of traveling in the sun and heat.

"He has a good resting place," I said. "Right near the Pecos River with a sweet gum tree for shade."

She smiled and descended the steps and took hold of my hands and asked me if I would walk with her and I said sure. She was taller than me and had flat bosoms. We walked for hours and did not return until the shadows had grown long in the yard. The pigs lay sleeping.

The old man and the woman invited me to stay for supper and I sat next to Fannie and we ate peas and chicken and boiled turnips and once, in the middle of me taking a bite of drumstick, I felt Fannie's hand just above my knee, the fingertips thrumming lightly, but kept right on chewing and holding conversation with the old man.

"I don't believe Tom ever mentioned you, Henry," the old man said. "Course, he hardly ever wrote home."

"Tom always said how someday he was going to pay a surprise visit," I said. "Maybe that's the reason he didn't write, he wanted to surprise you."

Fannie's fingers squeezed my thigh and something sweet trickled up my leg without my willing it to.

Tom's mother, who said her name was Mary, stared at her plate, the peas piled in one spot, a chicken wing untouched in another, the turnips by themselves.

"I'm sorry I had to deliver the bad news," I said, and she looked up at me, her lips pressed tightly together, then looked back down at her dinner plate.

"Tell me why that lawman shot Tom in the guts," the old man said. "I want to know what it was my boy did to make a lawman shoot him in the guts."

I lied of course. Bringing bad news was one thing, running Tom down in front of his kin was another.

"It was a mistake," I said. "Tom hadn't done anything worth getting shot over."

"Then why'd it happen?"

"That lawman was trying to kill me and Tom got in the way."

The woman looked up with her eyes without raising her head.

"I was wanted for stealing a rich man's cattle," I said. "Call that a crime if you want to, maybe it is."

The woman's eyes closed as if she'd died.

"You an outlaw, Henry?" the old man said.

"I guess in some quarters you could call me that."

"Tom? Was he an outlaw too?"

The poor woman's nose twitched like a rabbit.

"No, sir. The only wrong thing Tom ever done was get in the way of a bullet meant for me."

"Then he died something of a hero?"

"Yes, sir. You could say he did."

That seemed to ease the old man's mouth and set him to chewing again. Fannie's hand moved up between my legs and nestled there like a twitching sparrow.

Later the old man and I sat and smoked on the front porch and sipped liquor from a crock jug, his finger looped through the handle and resting on his shoulder. He said he was from Tennessee and that's how they drank liquor; it was all right by me however they drank it. He told me I could sleep the night in his lean-to out back of the house. It had begun to rain and for a time we sat there and smoked and drank liquor and watched the rain drip from the eaves. Every time it rained I remembered my mother. Rain, I've come to believe, is a womanly thing.

My mind drifted between the rain and the weight of Fannie's hand earlier at the table and how it had stirred me and how her fingers traced the rising hardness of my pecker. She wasn't dark or pretty the way I favor a girl to be, quite the opposite. She had crooked teeth that showed when she smiled. And flat bosoms never did do much for me. Her skin was washed pale.

I thought about just riding all night in the rain.

There in the lean-to, while I lay listening to the rain pattering off the metal roof, she came and crawled in my blankets and removed her bloomers and pressed up against me, and in spite of myself, I took her into my arms and let her tug down my britches.

"The first time I saw you," she whispered, "I knew."

I didn't say anything.

Her hands were cool and damp from the rain.

"What about your pap?" I said. "What if he finds you here with me?"

"He won't," she said. "He never leaves the bed once he's in it."

I closed my eyes and felt her hands closing around me, felt the flick of her tongue crossing my skin, and thought of a snake, or the way I've seen gila monsters use their tongues when they're searching for prey. Flicking and flicking over my skin leaving wet droplets like warm rain.

"Don't worry," she whispered, "I've been lonely a long time."

I didn't say anything. Maybe I should have. Tom lies in a cold grave lonely, only Charlie to keep him company.

My silence was her gift, my sacrifice for Tom, is the way I looked at it.

She slipped away sometime after the rain stopped, taking with her my seed and my silence. I never knew if the baby was born or if it died like the others.

Nature has no *cure for this sort of madness.* This I read in a book some years later.

27

TISN'T LIFE THAT MATTERS! TIS THE
COURAGE YOU BRING TO IT.
— SIR HUGH WALPOLE

I knew it was time to go.

I looked on the street below and saw myself as free as the Rio Bonito.

Bell had the flux, so he claimed, cramps, good god almighty!

Ollinger sat with his shotgun across his knees, one eye off slightly — a cockeyed man without a prayer only he didn't know it.

Garret came up the stairs, those long legs of his taking them two at a time. He entered the room and looked me up and down, his sugarloaf hat tilted to one side. Twisted lips, and bloodless face.

"Kid," he said, then poured himself a cup of coffee from a pot Bell had made but hadn't been able to drink because of his guts tied up in knots.

I saw three dead men.

"I'm going to White Oaks to purchase lumber for the scaffold," Garrett said to Ollinger.

"We could hang him from a tree and save the government money," Jolly Bob said. Garrett squinted over the steam of coffee and asked Bell if he was sick.

"Flux," Bell said. "Got the shits and the cramps."

Garrett eyed me over the tin cup.

"You fed this boy yet?" he asked Ollinger.

Jolly Bob belched.

"You feed him," Garrett said. "I mean it, Bob."

"I'll feed him these dimes I got loaded in this here shotgun," Jolly Bob said. Garrett gave him a sour look.

"I'll be back in a few days."

Bell scampered down the steps to the outhouse and came back after Garrett had left, holding his belly, but in the time he was gone Ollinger said, "You don't know how much I want to pull these triggers on you, Kid. Goddamn if it wouldn't make me feel good just to do it."

"Do it," I said. "Go ahead, Bob. Just pull them."

He thumbed back the hammers and I waited for him to go through with it. It would be a fast way out, better than a rope.

He lifted the shotgun and pointed it at me and sighted down the barrels with his off eye and I stood up to give him a better target.

"Go on, Bob. Do it."

I could feel the tick of my heart in my wrists.

The barrels wavered up and down with his

breathing, the air shrill through his nose.

And for a moment I thought he finally had some hair around his ass but he heard the door at the bottom of the stairs open and lowered the shotgun and had it resting across his knees again when Bell reached the upper rooms.

Old man Gauss brought me my breakfast on a platter and I found the note under a biscuit. Gauss couldn't write or read so it wasn't him who wrote it. All it said was: *Gun hidden in shithouse.* I ate the words with a cold biscuit.

Ollinger watched me and Bell played a game of monte with matchsticks for money till the clock struck the time as noon. Jolly Bob rose and said to Bell he was going across the street to get his dinner and I watched him go into the other room and heard him rack his shotgun, then tromp down the stairs, while beating Bell at a hand for twenty matchsticks.

"Damn, Kid, you should have been a professional gambler with your luck," Bell said.

"No luck to it, J.W. A lucky man is one who has a plan."

He rubbed his gut.

"Might as well me and you visit the privy," I said, and Bell said it sounded like a good idea to him.

"Be easier if you'd take off at least my leg irons," I said, but he wouldn't hear of it.

I found the gun just above the door on a jut of

frame, fully loaded, and tucked it in under my shirt. Then, with Bell trailing behind, I made the stairs two at a time, hopping like a rabbit, because I wanted Ollinger's shotgun with the double load of dimes.

Bell's jaw dropped when he saw the pistol in my hand.

He blinked and stuttered and looked like he wanted to grow wings and fly.

"Shuck these irons off me, J.W., and be quick."

But his fear had gotten the best of him, and *that* I hadn't counted on.

These were his last words:

"Jesus Christ, Kid, don't do it!"

I shot him when he bolted for the stairs and he flopped dead on the landing. He was the first man I ever regretted having shot.

I found Ollinger's shotgun and went to the east window and waited for him to come out of the Wortley, which he quick enough did, shading his eyes against the sun, a napkin still tucked in the top button of his shirt as he high-stepped it across the street.

"Hey, Bob," I said when he reached the yard below the window.

He looked up, saw me, saw the double-eyed shotgun.

"I'm killed," he said.

"Goddamn if you ain't, Bob."

I gave him both loads.

Life and death are simple matters. All you have to do is pull the triggers, or not.

I took so many pistols and rifles I couldn't carry them all. Stepped over Bell, his blood dripping like red paint down the steps. Poor Bell.

I told Gauss to fetch me a horse. Took him half an hour. Eyes peered at me from doorways. No one came. The law, what little of it there was, lay dead dead dead. I rolled a paper cigarette and smoked it while waiting for Gauss to catch a horse — a free man on the streets of Lincoln. No one came to stop me. They saw Jolly Bob and weren't inclined to join him.

The Rio Bonito sang me a song while I smoked and waited for Gauss to bring me a horse. When he did, I had him chop the chains with an ax that shot sparks with every blow.

"Gott damn!" He swore and sweated, striking and striking downward until I was busted free.

Gauss leaned on the ax and looked at me with wolf-yellow eyes.

"Gracias, amigo," I said and handed him my makings.

He answered me in German, then corrected himself and said, "Mein gott, you kilt them all!"

"They didn't bring enough to the game. You can tell Garrett that when he returns with his load of lumber for my scaffold. Tell him to use it to build those fellows coffins."

It was a long time before I ever went back to Lincoln. It was a bad place to be.

BOOK TWO

28

THERE IS DANGER EVERYWHERE, IN THE BLOOD, IN THE HEART, IN THE EYES OF WAITING LOVE.
— FROM THE JOURNAL OF HENRY MCCARTY

Manuella sits and stares at her birds and I wonder if she is still thinking of eating ice cream in the park the evening before and the bitter words that spilled from her mouth. She hardly looks at me, even as I sit across the table from her and spoon sugar into my coffee.

"You still want to see me dead?" I say. I haven't forgotten. I don't forget. Ask Garrett, ask any of them.

"Let's not talk about it, Henry," she says, her voice a thread.

"I don't know why not," I say. "What else do we have to talk about?"

She sniffs like she might be getting a cold.

"I was thinking about the time after you escaped from jail in Lincoln and came to my door," she says. "How did you know that I would take you in?"

"Is that what you want to talk about?"

She looks tired. It troubles me to think that she might die and leave me the last one alive. She is the last thread that ties me to this earth, the last living memory of crimson days and stark, sun-filled skies, of black mesas that finger out onto the tan deserts. The sage is blue silver and the Pecos and Bonito, the Canadian and Cimarron, are wet tongues that lick the dry land and the bones of the dead. Their memory is duller now, distant and growing more so every day. Manuella is the only living reminder, the only connection of flesh to the skeletons of the past.

"Yes, that is what I want to talk about," she says. "I want to know why you came to my door that day knowing the truth, knowing how I must have felt toward you over Charlie's murder."

I try to remember that day and the reason why I knocked on her door out of all the doors of women I could have knocked on. Now, in the dust of our years, she wants me to explain it.

"I went down to see Tom Mix yesterday," I say.

Her eyes are constantly rimmed red and I can see the small salmon spots on her nose where her reading glasses pinch.

"Whatever made you think I would ride away with you?" she says. "You were so wild and dangerous and I was still grieving."

"I knew Charlie," I say. "I knew how he was always talking about you, telling me and Tom how much he loved you, what a good woman you were, how he wouldn't even dance with another woman and was always writing letters to you. The way he carried on about you — I guess I just had to find out for myself."

"Did it make you jealous, Henry, Charlie's love for me?"

"Never been jealous of a thing in my life." But she knows a lie when she hears one.

She sips coffee from her saucer and watches me over the rim.

"You wanted to see if you could have me," she says. "That was the only reason."

"No, that's not true."

"Men like you," she says. "You must always try and get what you don't have, even if it is another man's wife."

"You weren't another man's wife," I remind her. "In case you forgot, Charlie was dead, you were a widow, not a wife," I say. "There's a difference."

"Not to you there wasn't," she says. "If Charlie hadn't been murdered, I suspect you'd have still tried to get me to ride away with you sooner or later."

"Ha, a lot you know."

"You don't fool me in the least, Henry. Never did, never will."

"You went, didn't you?" I say.

"You put too much sugar in your coffee," she says.

"Now who's changing the subject?"

"What do you write in that book of yours when you go into your room and lock the door?"

"Nothing," I say. To me it's a private matter.

"You see," she says, "that's the difference right there."

"What is?"

"Charlie never kept any secrets from me. But you, you've got a whole book full of secrets."

"Nothing secret about it," I say. "They are just thoughts I write down."

"But secret ones," she says.

"Have it however you please. Least I've not gone around for fifty years waiting for you to die just so I can be there to throw the first dirt down on you."

She looks at her reflection in the brown mirror of coffee. I shouldn't have said it.

"Charlie was an open book when it came to me," she says, her voice as fragile as a dream.

"You need to rest?" I ask.

She waggles her head.

"You are like a bottomless mine, Henry. Full of dark secrets and old bones. I never would allow myself to fall into your darkness and that has galled you over the years. I didn't fall under your spell like those empty-headed senoritas, like Celsa, even though she was married."

"I never cast my spell on any woman who didn't ask for it, including you," I say, for my own heart is grown bitter now.

"Death will not be kind to you, Henry. All the ones you killed, all the ones you've hurt — they "will all be waiting for you on the far side of the river."

"You still believe in all that nonsense?" I say. "Men rising up from death, the great hereafter? I bet you believe that Jesus was a Mexican too?"

Her lips seam together in a tight smile that is not a smile, as though she knows I'm such a fool that I need pitying.

"You'll see," she says. "You will see."

"I'm not worried," I say. "That same God that is waiting on me to answer for my sins is the one that made me in the first place. Any fault to be found, it will be his own."

"Have you ever felt sorry for the dead, for the ones you've killed, Henry?"

"What's done is done. Save your prayers for the living, they need them more than the dead."

"I was twenty-five years old when you came to my door that night, a young woman whose husband's blood stained your hands. I was wrong for having gone with you, but as you say, what's done is done."

"Charlie's been dead a long time," I say. "When are you going to let him go?"

"Never, Henry."

"Your heart isn't big enough for both of us, is it?"

She smooths her hair with the palms of her hands and weaves it into a black and silver rope.

"Listen to it rain," she says, her head bowed while she braids her hair. And for a moment she is the same beautiful young woman she was back then, the way she was the first time Charlie introduced us, with her head bowed, braiding her hair. The rain runs slick against the window, the little glass birds sit and stare with unblinking eyes at the wormy trails of raindrops.

I go to my room and take a book from the shelf and sit near the window where the light is at its best on such a sunless day and there I read this:

"Is there anyone there?" said the traveler,
Knocking on the moonlit door.
"Tell them I came and no one answered,
That I kept my word," he said.
Ay, they heard his foot upon the stirrup,
And the sound of iron on stone,
And how the silence surged softly backward,
When the plunging hoofs were gone.
— Walter de la Mare

I don't know why, but it seems to me that my life with Manuella has been the silence that surges softly backward. I take up my pen and write this now on the page of my journal, knowing someday she will read it and understand that it wasn't anything I or anyone else could explain that made me come that night and knock on her door and ask her to ride away with me. And from that day until this, it has always been the silence surging softly backward.

29

I COULD HAVE DANCED FOREVER WITH THE PRETTY BROWN GIRLS. BUT A BULLET IS FASTER THAN THE WIND AND FINDS THE HEART EVERY TIME. I RIDE MY DREAMS INSTEAD OF HORSES.
— FROM THE JOURNAL OF HENRY MCCARTY

"*Billy,* this is Manuella, my wife," Charlie said, rain frozen to our slickers after a long ride back from the Llano Estacado. Charlie had ice moustaches that dripped down his chin.

She was dark-eyed and was weaving her hair when we marched in, sitting at a table nearest the light, steam rising from her coffee cup. Looked at Charlie, then at me, bowed her head like she was praying, and wove her hair.

Charlie poured us each a cup of the hot coffee and I sipped and watched his wife while he pulled off his boots and wiped bits of ice from his moustaches.

"We did good over in Texas," Charlie said to her in that cheery way he had, but she acted as though we weren't even in the same room, weaving her hair in silence.

"Sold, what was it, Kid, two, maybe three hundred mavericks? Chisum's cows, he won't miss 'em a lick. Man's got a million cows, he ain't going to miss a couple of hundred."

I knew then, looking at her, that someday I would hold her hair in my hands, and when she looked up again she looked at me while Charlie stood in the corner with his back to us and shucked off his wet drawers. She looked at me for the longest time, as if she knew our destiny.

That night at supper I stole glances while Charlie slipped out the door to bring in some more firewood, while Charlie scraped the last of the beans out of the pot, while Charlie went to the window to look out at the weather.

"Ice," he said at one point. "Snow and rain is one thing, but I hate an ice storm like the devil, don't you?" Then he turned, but not in time to see me stealing glances at his wife.

That night I slept on the floor in front of the fire and could hear them in the other room, hear the way the husk mattress of their bed rustled, hear their whispers, her laughter, Charlie's grunts. It made me stare at the flames and see things I didn't want to see. The rainy ice clicked against the tin roof and the wind sang along the eaves and later I could hear them breathing steady and even and knew that Charlie had exhausted himself and her with his loneliness after a month on the Staked Plains while my own loneliness was a stalking wolf.

In the morning I awoke to see her standing at the stove with her back to me and she was wearing a pair of Charlie's trousers and a red wool shirt, both too big for her, and for the longest time I simply lay there with my eyes pressed to slits, peering at her, hoping she would turn around, but she never did.

Later me and Charlie attended the stock and broke the ice from their coats and fed them apples and Charlie said the bay wouldn't last until spring. Its ribs stood out like barrel staves against its rough hide. I said I'd shoot the pony for him but he shook his head no.

"She might make it and if she does, by God, I intend to ride her into Lincoln and get twenty dollars for her and buy Manuella that red dress in Tunstall's store."

I thought of her wearing the red dress.

Later, when Charlie made a trip to the outhouse after supper, I said to her, "Charlie's wanting that bay to live long enough to sell it and buy you a new dress."

She looked toward the door, then at me.

"Charlie is foolish with money," she said.

"You'd look pretty in it."

"If he saw the way you looked at me," she said.

"Someday I might look at you that way all the time."

She turned her back to me and washed the supper plate she was holding.

"If I said something to him," she said, "he would stop being your friend. He might even shoot you. He is a very jealous man."

"I'll give him no reason to do either," I said. "But maybe you will."

She stood stock-still for a moment, then turned and said, "Maybe I will."

I rode toward the sun the next morning while she slept with Charlie in his corn-shuck bed and I thought of the color of her eyes and the bitter fruit of a woman's loyalty to her lover.

Remembering it all now, I find a poem within one of the many books I've collected. A fellow named Swinburne wrote it and I found it one day in an old bookstore in Taos — a habit I'd acquired since meeting a woman in El Paso who owned a small shop with books and who went for a walk with me along the river. The book has a coat of dust on its cover:

> Thou hast conquered, O pale Galilean; the world has grown gray from thy breath:
> We have drunken of things Lethean, and fed on the fullness of death.
> Laurel is green for a season, and love is sweet for a day;
> But love grows bitter with treason, and laurel outlives not May.

I don't pretend to understand it all, but seems to me the parts of feeding on the fullness of death, and love being sweet for a day, speak of the life she and I've shared. And also the part of how love can grow bitter with treason says a lot about the fact that Charlie was always there between us, even in death.

I wonder if this fellow who wrote this ever rode a horse or threw a rope or shot a pistol in the face of another man. I wonder if he ever stole another man's woman, or had another man's woman steal his heart.

Seems to me he must have, because there is pain in his pen.

30

I WENT ALONG THROUGH LIFE AS WELL AS I COULD AND KISSED CLOSE THE EYES OF ENEMIES AND LOVERS ALIKE AND BADE THEM FAREWELL ON WHATEVER JOURNEY THEY WERE TAKING.
— FROM THE JOURNAL OF HENRY MCCARTY

I knew the moment Charlie brought him into our house that none of us would ever be the same again. I remember there was an ice storm and Charlie and Billy appeared to me like ghosts, the ice making their faces slick and white, the ice clinging to them as though they had risen from the dead and come to me in a dream.

Charlie had been gone nearly two months and I was not certain that he would ever return to me, or if he did, if it would be the law or a sheep-herder bringing me his body with his face bloodless, his arms folded across his chest.

"This is Billy" is what he said, as though I should drop everything and be happy that he had brought this wild boy to our home.

He dozes on the front porch now, the once

wild boy who is now an old man. I remember it as if it was only yesterday, the way the ice clung to his hair, the way his eyes never stopped watching me. Sometimes he dreams and talks in his sleep. I hear him calling out the names of the old ones: "Charlie, Tom, Garrett." He fidgets like a dog, his hands jerk, and his face twitches as the demons chase him through the hills of his dreams.

The first I noticed him really looking at me was when Charlie turned his back to remove his wet clothes in front of the stove. I felt myself shiver when I looked into the eyes of the one they called the "Englishman's Boy." I shivered as if the ice from his hair was falling on my skin. A woman knows what a man is thinking when he looks at her. If Charlie had seen him looking at me that way, that would have been the end of them. And maybe it would have been better if he had.

Charlie, whom I grew to love before I even knew what love was, stole my heart and innocence. Charlie, himself innocent of the deception by his friend, this boy he doted on and eventually gave his life for, would become Charlie my husband, my cold ash of memory.

I was just a girl when Charlie came to our house and sat on his horse and spoke to my father the first time. Me, a girl in a white dress who had only an hour earlier silently vowed to give her life to God in her room while on her knees, knowing that no man would ever want her. I heard my father and mother talking that night as I lay on my bed and counted the stars and asked God what *he* wanted of me.

My father told my mother, "That young man has come for our daughter," and my mother said simply, "No, she is too young to go with him," and Father told her that I was no longer a child and old enough to marry. "And besides," he said, "we could use the money this gringo is offering."

One day when my mother was washing my hair she looked at me and said, "I guess you are a woman now and cursed as all women are." Then she proceeded to tell me what to expect from men and it frightened me, the way she described what it was they wanted from a woman, what they demanded.

Charlie arranged it with my father to take me away with him to live in the house he had on the Rio Feliz. He came one day with a wagon and him and my father loaded it with my few possessions: a trunk that my mother gave me with her wedding dress in it, a spinning wheel she no longer used, a box of china with two chipped cups.

She made Charlie promise to marry me in a church before the leaves turned brittle on the cottonwood trees and the winds came down off the mountains cold.

It seemed like a long ride from our hacienda on the Rio Penasco to Charlie's small adobe on the Rio Feliz. It took nearly six hours and several times Charlie halted the wagon and helped me get down to stretch my legs. He was always talking, telling me what a good life we would have, talking about having children and chickens and someday a large herd of cattle. I wondered what it would be like to be the wife of a rich man.

The third time we stopped and he helped me down he said, "I would like to kiss you, Manuella, is that okay with you?"

It was a clumsy effort, very awkward, and his beard scratched my cheeks, but it made me feel womanly and I thought I suddenly understood all there was to know about my womanliness and the needs of a man. My mother had explained it and it wasn't so bad. Then the second time he kissed me he put his hand between my legs and pressed through my dress and I felt sinful and ashamed and without power to prevent him from doing whatever he wanted to do to me.

"You will be my wife soon," he said. "The Bible says we are to be of one flesh, that what is mine is yours and what is yours is mine." He lifted me into the back of the wagon and pushed up my skirts and looked at what was now his and no longer my own. I saw a cloud that was in the shape of a horse's head directly above me as Charlie's weight bore against me and I felt the first sharp pain of my deliverance. I watched the cloud change shape and become a sailing ship, then a turtle, and bore the pain, thinking of it as God's cross given to me as a woman, thinking this is what he must have wanted of me. Not his bride, but Charlie's. I don't remember how long it was before Charlie helped me to the front seat again and drove us on to his ranchero, but when we stopped again and I walked off a distance to squat behind a tree, I saw the blood there smeared over my thighs and thought that God had forsaken me just as he did Jesus. Charlie heard me crying and found me and said over and over again, "I'm sorry. I'm sorry."

I was braiding my hair. Earlier I had washed it in rainwater and had let it dry by the stove.

Then Charlie came in with this wild boy he called "Billy the Kid."

31

I HAVE TASTED BLOOD AND I HAVE TASTED THE SWEET MOUTH OF A WOMAN AND I TELL YOU THAT I LIKE THE TASTE OF A WOMAN'S MOUTH MORE THAN I DO BLOOD.
— FROM THE JOURNAL OF HENRY McCARTY

A bit of yellow light shone in the window there in the old hospital of Fort Sumner, as though she knew I would be coming for her. Mother used to say, "Leave a light in the window for the returning son." Arrived before dark, but squatted in the hills at a camp with ol' Yerba and his sheep who, under a half-moon, looked like clouds fallen to the ground, resting and baaing, their fat bodies not content with the peaceful night.

Yerba's brown face was wrinkled like a leather sack whose coins have been stolen, his eyes dark wet, the flames of fire in them as he squatted and roasted a leg of mutton and looked up when I rode into his camp.

"Hola," he said, and smiled with hardly any teeth left to him but one here and one there — enough to eat mutton and let you know he was happy.

The sky bled red to the west and was black silver toward the east. The North Star was where it always is.

"Amigo," I said, and squatted down beside him and took in the scent of his mutton, the leg irons still clapped around my ankles, the chains tied to my belt.

"You came into some trouble, eh?" he said.

"Sure, sure. Mucho trouble, senor."

"You want some mutton?"

"Si."

He pulled it from the fire and let me slice a nice juicy piece, then nodded to the jug of liquor he'd made from the hearts of agave, a thorny nasty plant, sunken to cool in the creek between two large rocks.

"You want me to cut those irons off your legs?" he said after the last of the mutton was in our bellies warm and heavy.

"Sure," I told him, "but first, let's have a smoke and tell me what you hear about Billy the Kid."

He rubbed his hands, for the nights were still cool, and held his palms to the flames.

"Ah, Chivato," he said. "I have heard that they hanged him down there in Lincoln. Garrett put a rope around his neck." Yerba shook his head while staring into the flames, his eyes greedy for their light.

"So he is dead?" I said.

"*Se le condeno a muerte,* he was condemned to

186

death. He was a good boy. Good to everyone, the Mexican people especially. They are already singing songs about him."

"Si, this I've heard too," I said.

"But, you know," he said. "They kill everyone who is good."

"Who does?"

He waved one of his hands toward the darkness.

"Them," he said. "Anyone who is his own man, *they* kill."

I handed him my tobacco and papers so he could roll himself a cigarette, for which he seemed very grateful.

"Did you know Billy the Kid?" I said.

He nodded, licked at the paper he'd funneled with tobacco, then rolled it and twisted off both ends before putting one end between his soft lips and letting it dangle there in a moment of expectant pleasure.

"Yes, I knew him. He came to my camp often and ate with me and drank some of my pulque."

"Then you've lost a good friend," I said.

"Oh, si. My heart is very sad. He is up there now with God."

I watched as he pointed a finger, brown and crooked as an ocotillo stick, toward the stars scattered across the tarnished sky and felt the wind on my neck as it did a ghost dance in the embers of the old man's fire.

"You think that's where he is, eh?" I asked. "Up there?"

"Yes. Up there. With God."

"Knock off these leg irons," I said, "and I will be in your debt, senor."

He had a cold chisel and a hammer that he used and soon had me feeling light again.

"You can keep them," I said, rubbing my scorched ankles.

"Why would I want leg irons?" he asked as I found my saddle and turned the little black mare Gauss had rounded up for me toward Fort Sumner.

"You can tell your friends that you gave Billy the Kid his freedom," I said. "And that he shared your mutton and pulque and that you smoked his tobacco. You can tell your friends that he's not with God — at least not yet."

He thought about that one for a minute, then bared what teeth he had.

"You are Billy?"

"Si."

He laughed as if I'd just told him a good joke, rubbed his palms over his knees, and leaned into the fire to light his cigarette.

"Vaya con dios, mi compadre."

"Be careful, hombre, the wolves might eat your sheep and Garrett might kill your friends." I told him this as I turned the mare's head down the slope toward Fort Sumner and the light shining in the window of the old hospital.

I could hear laughter from Beaver Smith's saloon as I knocked on Manuella's door and

188

waited. I would have liked to go where the laughter was and had a little fun and forgotten my recent troubles, but my ankles were raw from the leg irons, the skin scraped off and burning. I would have liked to dance but the weight of iron had made me weak in the knees.

I waited and knocked a second time, and then suddenly she was standing there, a lamp of yellow light in her hand, the flame trapped in her eyes.

"My God" was all that she said. I stepped past her into the room that was once hers and Charlie's after they moved from the ranchero on the Rio Feliz that failed to make him a rich man or her a rich man's wife.

She saw the way I limped but said nothing and did nothing.

"I know what you are thinking," I said. "That Garrett hung me in Lincoln, that the crows devoured my eyes, and the wind turns me round and round." She watched me carefully from behind the flame and touched the small silver cross hanging round her neck.

"I came because you were the one I thought about in jail," I said, the light glowing against the bones of her cheeks, one side of her face in shadow. It was not a total lie.

"You are not welcome," she said. "You cannot stay here."

"We both know better." I was too weary and sore to spend much time in conversation with her, though I'd thought for many days what I would say to her when I came back for her.

"Charlie will . . . ," she started to say.

"He's dead, remember?"

Her eyes were dark and wet and filled with flames.

The laughter from Beaver Smith's saloon was carried on the warm wind to our ears. Someone played a guitar and sang and it made me think of rain when it has been hot for a long time.

"Are you hungry?" she said at last.

"Yes, for many things."

"If they find you here . . ." She spoke as though her breath was not enough to sustain her.

"They won't find me here," I said. "Garrett knows I wouldn't be foolish enough to come back to my old stomping grounds. He will never look for me here and no one will tell him. Everyone here is either my friend or my enemy. My enemies are too afraid to say anything and my friends are too loyal to speak my name."

"There is water in there to wash your ankles with," she said, nodding to a room just off the one we were standing in.

"I came to take you with me," I said.

"Then you are foolish."

"We'll see."

She blew out the flame of her lamp and I heard her steps leading to another room. I wouldn't follow her. Not tonight. The only way it would work was if I didn't follow her, didn't show her any sign of weakness or need. Maybe it would take a day or two, but when she stopped walking away, she would be ready to go with me. A good vaquero knows how to break a horse without breaking its spirit.

In the dark I listened for her breathing but didn't even hear that.

Instead, I heard more laughter from Beaver Smith's saloon and thought of the moonlight shimmering on the Pecos as I pressed cold, wet cloths to my ankles and wished for once it had all turned out differently.

Charlie and Tom sleep in a grave dug for three.

Charlie, then Tom, then me.

The Pecos sings our song, sings our song.

Moonlight on water, water and wine turned to blood by the hand of Jesus, the Mexican who walks on water.

Garrett rides a pale white horse, his mind insane with lies, waiting, waiting.

The Pecos sings our song, sings our song.

The muddy Pecos sings our song.

32

OH JESUS, I'VE DONE THINGS I'M ASHAMED OF, AND THINGS I'M NOT. BUT MAYBE THE WORST THING I EVER DID WAS TO STEAL MANUELLA FROM HER CHARLIE.
— FROM THE JOURNAL OF HENRY MCCARTY

The laughter and music carried up from Beaver Smith's cantina on the night wind as the river sang gently beyond the Stone Garden. It was all the music left to me, that of the wind and that of the river, and it came to me nightly there in my rooms at the old hospital. Never had I felt so lonely. The floor was cold and earlier it had rained. From the upper room I could see as far as the Stone Garden's wall and I knew that just beyond it, a short distance up a path, was the grave of my husband, who they had laid next to O'Folliard, side by side in a silent grave. The one who should have been there with them was downstairs, moving about in an off-step limp, his eyes dark with watchfulness, the ring of his spurs pronouncements of his restless spirit.

Garrett had brought Charlie to me in the back of a wagon under a shroud of old tarp stinking of cow manure, the toes of his boots exposed, the heel half gone from one.

Garrett said, "I will give you money to buy him a suit of clothes and a new pair of boots for the burying," as if that would do it, make me forget that he had murdered my husband, had murdered our dreams, our unborn children. New boots on a dead man's feet would not make dreams reappear.

I never asked how it was that he had killed Charlie — dead is dead and all the asking would not change it. Garrett, such a tall man without warmth to his spirit. Nothing like Charlie, who laughed and laughed and took little serious. Charlie a child, Garrett a man who slayed the child in us all. The father lives, the son is dead, the spirit ascends into the unknown.

Then Garrett said, "He was wearing Billy's hat, I mistook him for the Kid."

So that was it.

"Too late, too late," Garrett said. "How was I to know it was Charlie and not Billy? We all shot at once — too late, too late."

Charlie's clouded eyes stared and stared when I pulled the tarp away. His lips were blue.

"He died in my arms," Garrett said. "He kept saying, 'I wish . . . I wish,' then expired."

Two bloody holes in his shirt — above the heart, below the ribs. I kissed his blue lips.

That's how it was. Garrett left twenty dollars in silver coins for burial clothes and a new pair of boots, then stalked across the street to the cantina. This began my hatred.

Suddenly there was a knocking at the front door. Sometimes the men who drank in Beaver Smith's came by and clumsily knocked on my door thinking I would answer and let them in because my husband was dead and I was alone. As though that was what I wanted, what I waited for every night with a light in my window. For some drunken man to come by and push up my skirts.

I tell you this so that you will understand why I did not answer right away. And when the knocking continued I went only to tell whoever it was to leave me alone.

He was standing there, smiling, without a hat and coatless. Wounded.

Something cold and dark ran through my soul at the sight of him. I expected he had gone to his death in Lincoln, where I'd heard they had him in jail awaiting hanging. But now he was standing in my doorway, smiling and saying how he'd come to take me away with him.

He limped and told me that it was because of the shackles they'd put around his ankles. He showed me his wrists where the skin had been scraped off. He had a pair of pistols in the waist-band of his trousers that he said he'd taken from his guards. I was scared of him. More scared of him than of the men who drank at Beaver Smith's.

I said a silent prayer and asked God for protection from him — he was a fire whose flame burned hot, wild, his feet unbound from the earth. But look at him now, an old man with dim eyes and sagging flesh who still limps from iron shackles and untold bullet wounds and weak bones. And age. Look at him now, sleeping in a chair on the porch with the sun against the backs of his speckled hands, his chest rising and falling like that of a bird whose wings are broken, unable to rise and fly away. Henry is like a wounded bird waiting for death, floundering, floundering till it comes.

Look at *Billy the Kid* now and tell me what you think of him — this old, old man who still dreams of himself as a handsome, brave boy unafraid of the world, who dreams of another woman he keeps locked away in that old, old heart of his as though I didn't know. In his room, late at night, I hear the scratching of his pen across dry pages — a "journal of private thoughts" he says, kept under lock and key in a desk beneath his shelf of books. He prides himself in having read so many books, something he says John Tunstall put him on to long ago, before that poor man was murdered and began a war that never ended for the one sleeping there in the sun.

Secrets. He covets secrets the way a rich man covets gold.

I knew that very night when he came to my door, his boots full of blood, that there were things about him he would never tell me, not even if I gave him my flesh — which is all a woman can give to a man besides her heart. But Charlie had taken my heart to the grave with him and Billy knew that. The keeper of my heart was never a secret between us. A woman has only one heart to give and I gave mine to Charlie.

"I have come to take you away with me" were his exact words that night.

What made him think I would go with him? And why did I end up doing so?

I wonder as I watch him there on the porch, his mind addled with things that no longer exist, his soft snores like the purring of an old cat.

I have come to take you away with me.
Come to take you away.

Billy dances at the end of a rope.
Garrett has a waiting grave.

From my room that night I heard the music from Beaver Smith's and saw the wall around the Stone Garden and waited for him to knock on the last door between us, knowing that there were no more rooms for me to hide in.

Billy the Kid.
Billy the Kid.

33

THE MEXES WERE ALWAYS BETTER TO ME THAN THE WHITES; I SEEMED TO BE OF THEIR BLOOD AND THEY OF MINE. I GUESS I UNDERSTOOD THEIR HARDSHIP AND ATE THEIR SALTY TEARS.
— FROM THE JOURNAL OF HENRY MCCARTY

Poe's appearance at Sumner had excited no particular observation, and he had gleaned no news there. Rudolph thought, from all indications, that the Kid was about; and yet, at times, he doubted. His cause for doubt seemed to be based on no evidence except the fact that the Kid was no fool, and no man in his senses, under the circumstances, would brave such danger.

— Pat Garrett

For three days she did not speak to me. I burned the spines off of cactus pads and split them open and rubbed the meat on my wrists and ankles to heal them. I drank in Beaver Smith's and watched from dark corners the faces of men as

197

they came and went. I rode my pony out into the sage until the air turned sweet. I rode my pony into the Pecos where the water touched its belly, always watching and waiting for Garrett and his killers.

I walked to the old cemetery and found Charlie and Tom's grave, the ground caved in slightly, a single wood cross with their names burned into it, the names misspelled but it didn't matter. The cross leaning away from the wind. I straightened it.

Manuella called this place the Stone Garden. I guessed, looking at it, it did seem like a garden full of stones with names scratched into them and worn near away by the seasons.

Yesidra Perez
Pedro Gomez
Javiar Lopez
Infant
Infant
Infant
Morales

Some were too weathered to read but I went around reading them anyway.

Juan Romero
Jesus Gonzales
Maria Hernado
Alberto Hernado
Infant

Infant
Infant
Tom O'Folliard
Charlie Bowdre

And soon they would add my name to the cross.

A lizard skittered along the adobe wall, the mud warm with sun, and behind it the Rio Pecos mourned their song.

Juanita Delgado
Ernesto Ramon
Wm. Morton
&
Frank Baker
(Slain by the Kid)
Lupe Sanchez
Infant

The river mourned their song.

"Charlie, you and ol' Tom are out of this life of travail," I said, plucking a wildflower and putting it in my lapel. "Be thankful for that. Maybe Garrett did you boys a favor and maybe he will do me one too. Charlie, I'm taking Manuella with me. And Tom, I told your daddy the news. He wept and so did your mother. Your sister wept too."

Mares' tails brushed the sky, a portent of bad

weather, yet I smelled no rain in the air, and if it did rain I would hold out my tongue.

"You lads are in a good place. Manuella calls this the Garden of Stones, says that it looks like all that this little patch of earth will raise are gravestones for the dead. You boys remember Celsa, Sabal's wife? She told me once she believed that Jesus was a Mexican and walked on water and I laughed and said, 'I'd like to see him walk across the Pecos.' Boys, I tell you, ain't nobody can walk across the Pecos. If they could I'd be the first to do it."

The sun was warm through my shirt and I squatted there at those boys' grave and rolled me a shuck and struck the match head off my spur and had a good long smoke with my pals.

"This life ain't much, boys, but it's all I've got, and if Garrett comes he will die or I will. Either way you'll have company. Hell, he ain't such a bad fellow, Garrett. Just misguided and set too low a price for his loyalty. If I kill him, I kill him, and if he kills me then that will be it."

I smoked the shuck down and ground it out on my boot heel, then spread the little bit of tobacco leavings on their grave; I heard the Mescalero Apaches believe it brings good luck to offer tobacco to the dead. Hell, who's to say.

"Manuella still loves you, Charlie. I think she always will. But she cannot stay and waste her life here, living a spare existence without a future, and her still in the flower of her youth. It would be some sort of sin, a pretty girl like that

200

not having a man to take care of her. So I will take her with me and see that she does not squander her beauty and grow to be an old maid, a woman who passes nightly before the windows where a light shines into darkness. If the tables were turned, I'd expect that you'd do the same for me."

Wind ruffled my hair like a loving hand and I stood and said, "That's about it, boys. I guess we will meet down the trail. Listen to me, I sound like some preacher believing that there is an almighty hereafter where we will all gather round and sing and dance, with the devil on the fiddle, and a Mexican that can walk on water."

The wind shifted round and I could smell the river.

Rita Tavareo
Jesse Weaver
Luis Salazar
Paulito Gutierrez
Infant
Infant
Hector Camacho
Octavio Ruiz
Infant

Seeds planted deeply in the Garden of Stones.

And beyond, the river mourns the name of the dead, singing, singing.

Garrett stalks the lonely hills on a ghost-white horse, his hands drenched in blood.

34

DESIRE IS A HORSE WITH BLIND EYES.
—FROM THE JOURNAL OF HENRY MCCARTY

We three went to Roswell and started up the Rio Pecos from there on the night of July 10th. We rode mostly in the night, followed no roads, but taking unfrequented routes, and arrived at the mouth of Tayban Arroyo, five miles south of Fort Sumner one hour after dark on the night of July 13th. Brazil was not there. We waited nearly two hours, but he did not come. We rode off a mile or two, staked our horses, and slept until daylight. Early in the morning we rode up into the hills and prospected awhile with our field glasses.

Poe was a stranger in the county and there was little danger that he would meet anyone who knew him at Sumner. So, after an hour or two spent in the hills, he went into Sumner to take observations. I advised him, also, to go into Sunnyside, seven miles above Sumner, and interview M. Rudolph, Esq., in whose judgment and discretion I had great confidence. I arranged with Poe to meet us that night at moonrise, at La Punta de la Glorietta, four miles north of Fort Sumner.

Poe went on to the plaza, and McKinney and myself rode down into the Pecos Valley, where we remained during the day. At night we started circling around the town and met Poe exactly on time at the trysting place.

— Pat Garrett

I feared that Garrett would kill us all and begged Billy to leave — in those days I called him Billy, but after we had left that country he asked that I call him by his given name, Henry. Back in those old days, he was Billy to me. Now he is Henry and sometimes I think if he had taken a job at the bank and worn a starched shirt and necktie and black shoes, a name like Henry would have fitted him well. As an old man now it fits him well. Henry dozes in the sun and in his wakefulness stares mightily with clouded eyes toward the unknowing.

"No, no," he said, "I will not run from Garrett. Let him come and kill me if he can. I don't think that he can."

He rode his pony in every direction watching for Garrett, saying that if he had to he would catch him in an ambush and kill him, just like Garrett had killed Tom and Charlie.

"Garrett's an old dog," Billy said. "I won't give him the opportunity to bite me."

He mistook my fear as concern for his life, for

203

he rode his pony out one day looking for Garrett and upon his return brought me wildflowers — Indian paintbrush, lupine, and some cliff rose he had picked along the way.

That night there was a dance in the plaza and he asked me to go with him. The music played so brightly that I went, my heart still dark with fear and loathing, the same heart I'd given to Charlie, the same one he took with him to the grave.

Billy was a fine dancer, he told me that before we went.

"I like dancing with the pretty senoritas," he said. He was wearing a red sateen shirt and a pair of clean denim trousers and had cleaned his boots and wetted his hair and combed it.

"I am sure that there will be many willing senoritas to dance with you," I said, determined that I would not be one of them.

"No," he said. "There is only one I want to dance with tonight."

I wanted to say to him, "Do you know how many times I have thought about finding Garrett myself and telling him that you are here in Fort Sumner?" If I had not had such hatred for Garrett, I might have found him and told him about Billy with the hope they might murder each other.

It was at this dance that Billy introduced me to Billy Barlow.

They were similar in every respect, except Billy Barlow was a darker hue than Billy and maybe an inch or two shorter.

Billy Barlow treated me courteously, bowing at the waist when Billy introduced us. He had a handsome face and devilish eyes.

Billy told me that Billy Barlow was a cattle thief and a very good one.

"I think he is from Mississippi," Billy said. "Seems to me that's where he's from."

I paid little attention to him beyond that, even when he would come around in search of Billy. And when I heard that Garrett had shot him in Pete Maxwell's house and claimed it was Billy, all I could think of was the holes of his devilish eyes.

In spite of my fear and loathing of him, Billy was a fine gentleman that night. He was carefree and danced happily, the heels of his boots clicking like castanets on the cobblestones as he whirled and twirled around me, never once taking his gaze from me. His sombrero hung by a leather string down his back and his hair was damp and lay in dark ringlets. In spite of myself, I felt his happiness flow through me. It was a curious time for me.

That night he slept on the porch, a pistol in each hand, waiting for Garrett. I rested upon my bed listening to the night, listening to the river curl along its banks from beyond the Stone Garden. Listening for Garrett, listening, per-haps, for Billy's footsteps on the stairs.

Every day he won me over more with his smile and efforts to be charming, and what I before had hated about him I found myself no longer hating, yet not quite trusting either. I knew that Charlie had been murdered because of Billy — that if not for his wanting to be like Billy, Charlie would still be my husband and perhaps we would have had children and grandchildren and a long life together.

But Billy was hard to hate completely, especially when he tried so hard to win me. One afternoon he came carrying a small black and white dog in his arms and seemed as happy as a child.

"Guess what I found?" he said, and without giving me a chance to answer he told me that the dog had been Tom O'Folliard's and had run away the night Tom was shot.

"His name was Buster," Billy said, rubbing the dog's knobby head. "I found him eating garbage in back of old man Chacon's house. Must have been five or six big dead rats out there he'd killed. But hungry as he was, he wouldn't eat a one — ate Chacon's garbage instead. I admire a dog who will kill a rat but won't eat it, don't you, Manuella?"

These were the things that eventually won me over to him — the way he could be so boyish and tender, the way so many things amazed him.

From the upper room I would sometimes see Billy with that little black and white dog walking toward the cemetery, Billy tossing an ocotillo stick for the dog to fetch, and the dog running between his boots, then jumping into his arms.

These were the things that won me over.

Sometimes I would find him alone, staring out one of the windows, and he would turn and his eyes would be brimming with tears.

These were the things that won me over.

I think back to it now, as I watch him through the window, his head tilted to one side, half asleep in the rocker, and realize that Billy won me over to him little pieces at a time, until he had won enough of me to convince me to go with him when the time came. I wonder sometimes if he would have left that territory if I had not agreed to go with him. I wonder if I had stayed whether Billy the Kid would have been the one Garrett shot that night instead of a pretty good cattle thief named Billy Barlow.

35

I THINK IF IT WERE POSSIBLE, I WOULD SHOOT THE MOON TO PIECES.
— FROM THE JOURNAL OF HENRY MCCARTY

I then concluded to go and have a talk with Pete Maxwell, Esq., in whom I felt sure I could rely. We had ridden to within a short distance of Maxwell's grounds, when we found a man in camp and stopped. To Poe's great surprise, he recognized in the camper, an old friend and former partner, in Texas, named Jacobs. We unsaddled here, got some coffee, and, on foot, entered an orchard which runs from this point down to a row of old buildings, some of them occupied by Mexicans, not more than sixty yards from Maxwell's house. We approached these houses cautiously, and when within ear shot, heard the sound of voices conversing in Spanish. We concealed ourselves quickly and listened; but the distance was too great to hear words, or even distinguish voices. Soon a man arose from the ground, in full view, but too far away to recognize. He wore a broad-brimmed hat, a dark vest and pants and was in his shirt sleeves. With a few words, which fell like a murmur on our ears, he went to the fence, jumped it, and walked down toward Maxwell's house.

— Pat Garrett

I knew Garrett would be coming. Every day I rode my pony out in different directions and watched for him, hoping I would spot him and his bunch of ambushers. I wanted him to come. I wanted to end it right there in Sumner where it had begun. Either I would kill him or he would kill me, made no difference to me at the time.

Manuella was won over, but not as easily as I thought. She resisted me as long as any woman, I suppose, whose heart is set against you. Yes, she would go with me to the dances. Yes, she would sometimes smile, like the time I found Tom's dog and brought it home. But she maintained her distance from me, her heart given, I knew, to Charlie, who could not know that she still loved him unless there is more to death than any of us realize.

For weeks I slept on the porch with my pistols clutched to me, waiting for Garrett, knowing how much he liked to ambush a man, while Manuella slept alone in her bed in the upper floor of the old hospital — a place I much despised.

Billy Barlow came around quite a bit wanting me to go with him to steal some of John Chisum's cattle. I told him about the colored Chisum kept on who owned a big buffalo gun and could hunt men in the dark and shoot them from a mile off. Billy didn't believe me.

"Ain't no nigger can shoot no gun from a mile off and kill a man," he said. "Ain't no nigger can hunt a man in the dark either." I didn't argue with him for I had my own doubts that any man could do those things. But if any man could, it would probably have been Chisum's colored.

Billy and I played monte and drank mescal in Beaver Smith's. Billy Barlow might have been a pretty good cattle thief, but he was a poor hand at cards and could not drink worth a damn. I watched him lose his hat, shirt, and boots one night in a card game and walk out into the hills barefooted because he'd also lost his horse and saddle in that same game. I had some extras and rode out to his camp, which was just outside of Fort Sumner, and gave them to him the next day. He was surprised the boots fit his feet (we both had small feet) and danced a jig in them once he'd put them on.

"Thanks, Kid, I won't soon forget your kindness," he said.

I tossed him my old sombrero and a stitched rawhide vest and said, "It's not decent for a man to go around without a good hat on his head."

He put them on and grinned. It caused me to remember the last time I'd given my hat to someone. Charlie was killed wearing my hat — Garrett claiming he thought it was me because of the hat.

Billy Barlow, grinning, grinning, till Garrett put a bullet in him.

I remember not the day precisely, but the night was awash in moonlight. When Manuella and I arrived home from the dance the entire room of the old hospital was filled with silver light. I started to strike a lantern when her fingers touched the back of my wrist, the match still in my hand, unlit.

"What is it?" I said, thinking maybe she had heard something, danger perhaps.

"There is enough light already," she said and took my hand and led me up the stairs to the room where she slept. There the moonlight angled through a window that opened to the west in the direction of the cemetery where Charlie and Tom slept peacefully waiting for the end of eternity.

My friends sleep in moonlight.
Sleep, sleep, forever sleep.

She wore a simple blouse of white cotton with a string that tied the bodice and it took no effort at all to release it and slide the blouse off her shoulders, her skin a supple copper.

"Like this?" I said.

"Like this," she said and guided my hand to her breast. It was warm and I could feel the tick of her heart.

"Are you sure?" I said.

She lowered her eyes.

"No, I am not sure, but this is what you want."

I turned her gently until moonlight fell upon her face, then kissed the hand that held mine to her breast.

"No," she whispered, but this time did not walk away into the shadows and after that I slept no more on the porch.

Billy Barlow asked if I would sell him Tom's dog.

"I'd like that dog," he said. "I'll give you a dollar for him."

"He belongs to a friend of mine," I said, "dead, beyond that wall yonder," and pointed to the cemetery where Tom and Charlie lay until the Pecos flooded one time and carried them off. "I wouldn't feel right selling him."

"I'll make it five," Billy Barlow said. "He can ride up on the saddle with me."

"He kills rats," I said, "but doesn't eat them."

"Goddamn," Billy said in amazement. "I'll give you ten if you'll sell him." And so I did. I sold Tom's dog to Billy Barlow for ten dollars because I had no money and even less need of a dog.

I awakened in the morning to the sound of a rooster crowing, Manuella asleep in the bed next to me as if she was a dream I was having, her bare brown shoulders exposed to the early light. *Charlie's woman*, I thought. She would always be that and I knew it, her heart gone with him to the grave and beyond. But what remained was mine, I'd claimed it and claim it still even though I don't love her in the way that's right for a man to love a woman. Ours was a bond of need more than it was of love, but sometimes need turns into love and love into need. I'm not sure ours ever did, ever will. We seemed the only ones left from Garrett's guns.

Too quick we grow old and before
We know it, the time has fled
Never to return to give us another
Chance at youth and undreamt dreams.

Once you cross the Pecos they say you can never return — and for me, she was a river that you only crossed once. That very morning I arose from Manuella's bed and dressed, then walked to the cemetery and confessed what I had done as the sun burned off a fine morning mist.

"She's mine now, Charlie."

The river sings,
The river sings.

A viper's tongue singing,
The stench of Garrett on the wind.

"I will go with you," she said, "but only if you leave before he comes."

I told her I planned to kill him or be killed, that I would not leave Sumner until it was finished. She pointed to the cemetery wall.

"Then you will join them," she said. "Charlie and Tom."

I didn't care but I didn't believe it either.

Her tears fell on my hands and she said I'd turned her into a whore. And so we left two days before Garrett and McKinney and Poe arrived and killed Billy Barlow — a pretty good cow thief whose misfortune was none of my own.

36

ALL THE WORDS IN THE WORLD CANNOT TELL THE TRUE STORY OF EVEN A SINGLE LIFE.
— FROM THE JOURNAL OF HENRY MCCARTY

When the Kid, by me unrecognized, left the orchard, I motioned to my companions, and we cautiously retreated a short distance, and, to avoid the persons whom we had heard at the houses, took another route, approaching Maxwell's house from the opposite direction. When we reached the porch in front of the building, I left Poe and McKinney at the end of the porch about twenty feet from the door of Pete's room, and went in. It was near midnight and Pete was in his bed. I walked to the head of the bed and sat down on it, beside him, near the pillow. I asked him as to the whereabouts of the Kid. He said the Kid had certainly been about, but he did not know whether he had left or not. At that moment a man sprang quickly into the door, looking back, and called twice in Spanish, "Who comes there?" No one replied and he came on in. He was bareheaded. From his step I could perceive he was either barefooted or in his stocking-feet, and he had a revolver in his right hand and a butcher knife in his left.

He came directly toward me. Before he reached the bed, I whispered, "Who is it, Pete?" but received no reply for a moment. It struck me that it might be Pete's brother-in-law, Manuel Arbreu, who had seen Poe and McKinney, and wanted to know their business. The intruder came close to me, leaned both hands on the bed, his right hand almost touching my knee, and asked in a low tone — "Who are they, Pete?" — at the same moment Maxwell whispered to me. "That's him!" Simultaneously the Kid must have seen, or felt, the presence of a third person at the head of the bed. He raised quickly, his pistol a self-cocker, within a foot of my breast. Retreating rapidly across the room he cried, *"Quien es? Quien es?"* ("Who's that? Who's that?"). All this occurred in a moment. Quickly as possible I drew my revolver and fired, threw my body aside, and fired again. The second shot was useless; the Kid fell dead. He never spoke. A struggle or two, a little strangling sound as he gasped for breath, and the Kid was with his many victims.

— Pat Garrett

216

When I heard that Garrett had killed Billy the Kid I looked at Billy and said, "Did you know that Pat murdered you last week in Fort Sumner?"

He simply smiled and said, "No."

We both wondered for a time who it was that Pat Garrett had killed in Pete Maxwell's, then Billy said, "My guess is, a Mexican. Garrett could kill a Mexican easy and say it was me. No one would argue with him. They would be afraid of Pat, and those who weren't would be afraid of me. No, no one would say it wasn't me he killed."

He seemed more curious about it than troubled, guessing names of who it could have been that Garrett murdered, then finally said, "It must have been poor Billy Barlow. He is the only one without kith or kin in Sumner, the only one nobody would miss or mourn."

I remembered this boy with the devilish eyes and pleasant manners from the dance that night Billy introduced us. There were a few times he would come in search of Billy and once bought Tom's dog from him and would ride around Sumner with the dog perched on the pommel of his saddle. Billy said it was just poor luck on Billy Barlow's part.

Once he had it figured out, Billy seemed no longer concerned about the matter except for what he called Garrett's notorious deceit.

"Pat's mouth is full of lies and someday he will pay for his sins against me and Charlie and Tom.

I don't forget. I never forget." That was the last he spoke of the killing, except to say he was disappointed that Pedro Maxwell would have a hand in it. This I understood, because I knew that Billy had kept company with Deluvina Maxwell, one of Pete's daughters, and he saw Pete now as a betrayer. Billy had kept the company of many young women in Sumner; this I knew from when I was married to Charlie and Charlie would almost brag to me about the number of senoritas and senoras "the Kid" was intimate with. One was Celsa Gutierrez — Pat Garrett's own sister-in-law who was married to a man with a large herd of sheep. Charlie told me that when Celsa's husband was out in the hills with his sheep Billy would come and stay with her, that of all the many women he knew, Celsa was his favorite in Fort Sumner. I wondered, when I heard all this terrible news, whether she was still his favorite.

He reads his newspaper and sits in the sun. Who knows what thoughts go through his head? Who knows what words he writes in his book late at night, the pen scratching, scratching, across the dry paper?

I was never jealous of him over those other women, but a man who gives himself to one woman should not constantly have it in his head that he is making love to ghosts, writing letters to the dead. It is not respectful of the living.

In all the years, we have never once said the words "I love you" to each other. That is his only honesty with me, the only secret that he does not keep from me — that he does not love me. And I do not love him because of it. But without him, my life would be as empty as it was after Charlie was murdered. All these years together, you see, they count for something — they are what I know and what I've become. Henry's wife. Charlie's woman. A Mexican girl who was once pretty but now grown old who stares at glass birds and the brown speckled hands of an outlaw.

I see him dozing in the warm sun and wonder if he will awaken, or if I will one day find him dead, his lids half closed, milky eyes staring, his hands flaccid and ever still, the hands that held me when I was a young woman and sought the comfort of my flesh. Those hands that murdered so many, cold and incapable of harm, dotted with the brown spots of rot.

At times I think it would be a relief to me to find him dead in his sleep. But other times it brings a pain that angles sharply through my heart like the bent blade of a knife to see him like this, this once wild and faithless boy, now an old, old man with dim eyes and a head full of secrets.

I move about in this small Anglo house and sip my coffee and stare at my birds and wonder what God had in mind when he created us:

Manuella and Billy the Kid.

And this I write on my heart without pen or paper scratching:

Love unspoken
Death unbidden
This our due
for lives well hidden.

37

**DESIRE THIS, DESIRE THAT, IT DOESN'T MATTER, EVEN IF YOU GET IT.
— FROM THE JOURNAL OF HENRY MCCARTY**

Maxwell had plunged over the foot of the bed on the floor, dragging the bed-clothes with him. I went to the door and met Poe and McKinney there. Maxwell rushed past me, out on the porch; they threw their guns down on him, when he cried: "Don't shoot, don't shoot." I told my companions I had got the Kid. They asked me if I had not shot the wrong man. I told them I had made no blunder, that I knew the Kid's voice too well to be mistaken. The Kid was entirely unknown by either of them.

It will never be known whether the Kid recognized me or not. If he did, it was the first time, during all his life of peril, that he ever lost his presence of mind, or failed to shoot first and hesitate afterward. He told several persons about Sumner that he bore no animosity against me, and had no desire to do me injury. He also said that he knew, should we meet, he would have to surrender, kill me, or get killed himself. So he declared his intention, should we ever meet, to commence shooting on sight.

— Pat Garrett

Manuella read the *El Paso Times* and said, "Garrett's killed you in Fort Sumner."

Why didn't I feel dead if that was true?

That was then, two weeks after it happened. A year later I bought a copy of Garrett's book about me and read what you see here. If that's not proof it was poor Billy Barlow he killed and not me, I don't know what is. Read it for yourself. First he says he thought it was Pete's brother-in-law, then he says he knew it was me all along because of my voice. Me speaking in Spanish, something he didn't know much of. He admits I wouldn't be such a fool as to walk into a room with a stranger and not pull the trigger. He says he recognized me in a dark room, but that I did not recognize him. Well, hell, I'm not going to argue the point, you judge for yourself.

But that's long in the past. I can tell you this: Billy Barlow never stole another one of John Chisum's beeves nor was ever seen in that country again.

Buried him right there with Charlie and Tom at sunrise is what I heard. Dressed in white linen, a handkerchief over his bloody mess of a face, the women weeping while Poe and McKinney squatted in the dust still not convinced.

Sometimes I awake seeing Garrett's face in my dreams, awake with a start, my heart pounding, reaching for my pistolas, which aren't there. Not on the hips of an old man in his rocking chair — just pockets of lint.

But where was I?

Yes, in El Paso, the border hot that time of year, and from our small apartment we could see the Rio Grande and smell sweet peppers on the wind that came across from south of the river. Manuella naked, her skin damp, wearing pins in her hair because of the heat and wanting to keep it off her face and neck. Smooth and brown upon the bed as I'd imagined her the first time Charlie introduced us. Dark aureolas around her nipples, dark as chocolate rings. But I've lost my sweet tooth for her and even the sight of her uncovered does not stir my passion now.

The newspaper unfolded on the bed next to her, she ate an apple as she read and I thought that she could be posing for an artist, like one of those paintings you see over the back bar in the Coney Island Saloon.

Me already restless, not sure of what I wanted or where I wanted to go. Not sure if I had done the right thing by asking her to come with me. Just two weeks gone from Sumner and already itching for something to happen. But there she was upon the bed, naked and vulnerable and no place to go if I left her. All of Sumner would know she'd become Billy the Kid's whore if I sent her back. To remain in El Paso alone would mean she would have to work in the saloons and sell herself to men for the price of a meal. She'd known two men in the span of twenty years and I was one of them; I owed her something.

I asked her to call me Henry after we'd left Sumner and landed in El Paso. "Henry what?" she said. I told her Henry McCarty, my given name. She said it several times to herself as we walked along the Rio Grande on a warm evening and I liked the way it sounded coming from her, the way her Spanish sweetened the words of my name.

I had several hundred dollars saved from what Susan McSween had given me and wasn't in any hurry to take up crime, or honest work. I was a fair hand at monte and spent my evenings in the gambling halls while Manuella sat on the veranda of our hotel and waited for the sun to drop and the wind to come up from the river to cool her skin.

We slept late and I bought a new suit of clothes and her a red dress — the one Charlie never got around to buying that year because the horse he'd hoped to nurse to health and sell for the money died of the colic and Charlie of a bullet.

We window-shopped and ate all our meals in restaurants and I think that she became accustomed to the good life, the kind only rich men and bandits know the pleasure of. But even rich men and bandits must steal again if they are to continue enjoying such a world. I grew restless under the ceaseless sun of El Paso and even Manuella's embraces could not keep me content for long. There was too much fire in my blood — the peacefulness made me weak and left me wanting.

This is where I bought my first book — in El Paso on one terribly hot day.

There was a white woman who sold antiques, and among the lot she had a cart of books. Idle in my thoughts, I stopped in only to see if perhaps I could find a small brooch or jeweled pin to take to Manuella. The night before I had won nearly two hundred dollars in a game of cards and felt generous.

The woman was tall and refined and wore a shimmering green dress trimmed in black velvet; her skin was as white as milk and her hair as golden as honey, and I was immediately taken with her.

She was waiting on a man and his wife who were looking at an old table that seemed to me hardly worth selling. But I overheard the man say he wouldn't go higher than five hundred dollars for it. I heard her say the table was from the palace of a French king. This is when I saw the rack of books and amused myself thinking that maybe a good book was a thing worth buying. John Tunstall had a room full of books before Morton and the others shot him in the face. For some reason I decided that maybe I should own books, that they might be a good thing for a *dead* man to own — a man retired by Garrett's bullets from a wild life!

The books were musty and heavy and cool in my hands and I liked the feel of them immediately. I thought, rather than buy one, I might buy two or three. The names *Shakespeare* and *Hawthorne* and *Browning* were engraved on the spines — these names I had seen on the shelves of Tunstall's library. Sometimes I would see him reading by the firelight, his lips moving soundlessly.

I took them all and stacked them on the counter and waited. When the woman finished her business with the man and his wife she came over to where I stood and looked at the stack of books.

"All?" she said.

"All," I said.

She seemed pleased and smiled.

"Will you go for a ride with me along the river?" I asked.

"I don't know anything about you," she said.

"I like books," I said. "What more do you need to know?"

I rented a rig — a hack, and a bay to pull it — and helped her into it later that afternoon, the sky the color of brass and the air warm and still. We rode to the river where the air was cooler. She said her name was Yvette and that she was

French and had moved to the West as a young girl under her father's care.

"He was a dentist," she said. "He was murdered by a man for pulling the wrong tooth."

I said I knew what it was to have people you cared about murdered and told her about Charlie and Tom and some of the others.

"It is such a violent place, America," she said.

I asked why she stayed, why she didn't go back to France if she felt that way.

"Oh, but it is exciting and wonderful too," she said. "I could never leave such a wonderful place now."

I skipped rocks for her across the Rio and the wind fluttered the ribbons of her hat.

"Will you read all those books?" she said. "Or did you buy them just to impress me?"

"I know how to read and write, but I've never done much more than I've had to. I figured it is about time I owned some books."

"The one by Browning is lovely," she said. "So is Shakespeare — the sonnets especially. I am not very fond of Hawthorne."

I told her about Tunstall and how he liked to read and had a whole room full of books and how sometimes he would lend me one to read, which I did before the trouble began. She asked me what I did for a living and I told her I stole cattle and robbed banks. Her eyes grew wide as saucers, then I laughed and said I was only fooling — that I'd never robbed a bank, though I'd considered it a time or two.

"You are charming," she said.

"Yes'm, I know."

"Do you have a lady friend?" she asked. "A wife somewhere?"

I thought about Manuella. She was not my wife in any legal sense, though she'd taken my last name — McCarty — and not exactly my lady friend. It seemed too complicated to try and explain so I simply said, no, I had neither.

That seemed to please her and she put her arm through mine as we walked.

With her I felt much the same as I had when I was with Isabella — both of them refined women of good breeding and me but a poor drifter, cow thief, and killer.

We watched the sun go down; it seemed to drown itself in the waters of the Rio — a fiery orange ball melting into muddy water — and I drove her back to town feeling more sorry than ever that I'd taken Charlie's wife for my own.

Her name is under the heading in my book, *A Carriage Ride in El Paso* — a collection of black curls of ink that stain the page and my memory still. I have read all the books I bought from her that day, and whenever I pick up certain ones — Shakespeare, Hawthorne, Browning, I think of Yvette and the Rio Grande and the way the evening sun drowned itself and left us staring into shadows of silence.

I wrote this below her name:

Give me my robe, put on my crown; I have
Immortal longings in me.

This from the book of Shakespeare I purchased from her that day. My desire for having
what I do not have will always be my *immortal
longings* as long as I live, and maybe beyond the
grave.

38

DECEIT HAS KILLED MORE MEN THAN BULLETS.
— FROM THE JOURNAL OF HENRY McCARTY

In El Paso, Henry grew restless.

I showed him my nakedness and it was not enough.

He stood by the window staring, me on the bed undressed and waiting for what, I did not know.

His eyes never ceased their movement, his hands never still for more than a moment.

The heat in El Paso was ungodly.

He thought I did not know that he went with a white woman for a ride by the river and spent time with her there. But a woman knows when a man she lives with is unfaithful. He is different when he comes home, his deceit is written on his face, scented on his breath, spelled out in his touch. He came home late and brought me a garnet pin — "a small gift." He said his luck had been good at the card tables. I knew he was trying to purchase his sin. He had books.

By the river the air is cooler, but he took her there and not me.

Once I walked by the shop where she worked and looked in the window, the sun so bright it was hard to see beyond my own reflection. She was tall and elegantly beautiful and I could see why he would want her — she was so much unlike him. A man wants his opposite in a woman.

Charlie's hands were never graceful when he touched me. But my mother taught me to care for a man with the same gentleness I would for an infant. "Men are like babies sometimes," she said. "You must care for them and clean up their messes and not fret so much as to whether they love you or not. You will get only a little of what you want or need from a man, but as a woman, you must learn not to want or expect too much from them. None of them are perfect — God knows."

I asked her about my father and she said that he was a saint except that he wasn't a very good lover. I asked her if she'd had many lovers by which to judge him and she only smiled at me and turned her face toward the window of light above the sink. Charlie was my first man and Henry was my second. To Charlie I gave my heart, but to Henry I gave everything else, for his hands were graceful and he knew much about pleasing a woman — pleasure that brought with it guilt and shame, but pleasure I could not deny myself. I stared at the gringa through the glass and felt myself grow angry to think that Henry had given her the same pleasure he had given me, that his hands had glided smoothly over her breasts and hips, that his lips had kissed her.

Last week when he walked down to the fairgrounds saying that he might go see Mr. Tom Mix, I went into his room and found the key to his desk hidden under his pillow and looked in his book — the one he writes in late at night, the one that makes his scratching pen sound like mice nibbling on wood — and read her name in it. He had written on the first line: *A Carriage Ride in El Paso*, and under that her name: *Yvette*. I read what else he had written.

I took a French lady on a carriage ride down to the Rio. She was very pleasant to be with and reminded me a great deal of Isabella, the true love of my life. How I miss Isabella. We walked by the river and the air was cool and distinct and from the other side we could see the lights coming on in the little haciendas and hear the laughter of children and the evening church bells ringing for the Mass. She told me that her father was killed by a man because of a tooth and I told her about Charlie and Tom and how Garrett had killed them in the span of three days. I told her how he had killed me too, and when I did she touched my cheek. I skipped stones across the water for her and she tried it herself but could not skip a single one. I laughed and took her hand in mine and tried to show her how to skip stones, but still she couldn't manage it and for this I felt a deep affection toward her. She asked me if I had a wife or a sweetheart and I told her that I did not because I didn't want to spoil such a fine evening with talk of another woman. I am sorry now that I took Charlie's woman — sorry for her, sorry for me. But I keep my word and I will keep Manuella for as long as she wants to be kept. I have nothing more to say about that night except that I drove her back to town and thanked her for going with me on a carriage ride. I never saw her again except in my mind. I am going to talk to Manuella about going to Niagara Falls. I would like to see water. El Paso is so dry and full of sun and the dust coats my tongue. Mother told me that when it rained to stick out my tongue, and every time it rains I do. Maybe I was born of water. Some are born of fire, some of wind, but I am sure that I am of water.

I almost think that he wanted me to find it, wanted me to know that he once took a carriage ride down to the river with a white woman while I lay naked and alone waiting for him. Why else would he make it so easy for me to discover his secrets after all this time? But in truth, I knew about her the very next day. Why did he have to write about her and put her name in his book?

I think of my mother and her many lovers that

she refused to tell me about and wonder how, out of all of them, she came to marry my father — a selfless, dark-eyed man forever brooding. A man who would strike a deal to sell his daughter to a gringo. What was it that my mother saw, of all her many lovers, in this man who so easily sold his children to strangers?

But then I realize that perhaps she had no lovers until after she'd married. Maybe it was only then, when she took lovers, that she came to regret marrying my father. I'll never know these things.

In El Paso, Henry stood by the window and waited for rain.

He said, "If it doesn't rain soon we will leave here."

I was content with the life we had but Henry was restless and would often leave our bed in the middle of the night and not come home for hours.

Then one day he came and said, "Let's go to New York — I want to see all that water at Niagara Falls."

Yes, I thought. Anything to be away from the tall, handsome white woman. In spite of myself, I'd grown jealous.

So we went.

39

REMEMBERING IS EASY, FORGETTING IS HARD.
— FROM THE JOURNAL OF HENRY MCCARTY

On the following morning, the alcalde, Alejandro Segura, held an inquest on the body. Hon. M. Rudolph, of Sunnyside, was foreman of the coroner's jury. They found a verdict that William H. Bonney came to his death from a gunshot wound, the weapon in the hands of Pat F. Garrett, that the fatal wound was inflicted by the said Garrett in the discharge of his official duty as sheriff, and that the homicide was justifiable.

The body was neatly and properly dressed and buried in the military cemetery at Fort Sumner, July 15, 1881. His exact age on the day of his death, was 21 years, 7 months, and 21 days.

I said that the body was buried in the cemetery at Fort Sumner; I wish to add that it is there to-day intact. Skull, fingers, toes, bones, and every hair of the head that was buried with the body on that 15th day of July, doctors, newspaper editors, and paragraphers to the contrary notwithstanding.

Some presuming swindlers have claimed to have the Kid's skull on exhibition, or one of his fingers or some other portion of his body, and one medical gentleman has persuaded credulous idiots that he has all the bones strung upon wires. It is possible that there is a skeleton on exhibition somewhere in the States, or even in this Territory, which was procured somewhere down the Rio Pecos. We have them, lots of them in this section. The banks of the Pecos are dotted from Fort Sumner to the Rio Grande with unmarked graves, and the skeletons are of all sizes, ages, and complexions. Any showman of ghastly curiosities can resurrect one or all of them, and place them on exhibition as the remains of Dick Turpin, Jack Shepherd, Cartouche, or the Kid, with no one to say him nay; so don't ask the people of the Rio Pecos to believe it.

— Pat Garrett

The only showman of ghastly curiosities I know is Garrett. He shot poor Billy Barlow that night with a notched bullet and said it was me — face all gone, the poor fools believed him, the rest held their tongues and swallowed the secret. Garrett was a killer and he would murder anyone who opposed him, make no mistake about that.

He wrote his own history, the way he would have you eat it.

One man had my head in a jar of brine and charged a quarter to view it. Another my finger in a box and charged a dime. Toes and belly buttons if they could. Surprised they didn't sell my pecker for a dollar. Put it on a string like a chili pepper.

I still got everything I was born with: pecker, toes, fingers, and head. Unwashed by the Pecos and carried away like poor Charlie and Tom and Billy Barlow. Dig a hole and find me in it, and I'll say what Garrett said, that he killed me that night in Maxwell's with a lucky shot to the breast. Damn good shooting, you ask me. One through the heart in pitch black.

A motor car disturbs my rest.
Sun dapples through the trees
& lays an arabesque upon the walk
where children dance on outlined squares
of chalk and hop and skip and jump happily
to the tunes that play in their merry heads.

I got word Joe had died in a hotel alone, or did I mention that already? He wanted to whip Antrim's ass for taking Mother from us and I was willing to pitch in and help him. Now he's died, alone, alone, and I can't help him anymore. I wonder did he think of me in that last hour, or had the whiskey fogged his mind or the hatred clouded his thoughts and left him pitching

through the long dark into death's cold arms?
Alone, alone.

Manuella and I stood on the veranda of our
hotel and watched the great falls plummeting,
plumes of mist rising in the air like fog or horses'
breath on a frozen morning. All that water
rushing felt as though it washed away the grime
of my history and for a time I was unbound, free
and floating, happy again. I never saw so much
water.

The first night we went out onto the veranda
and saw the electric lights and heard the roar of
the falls and could see them illuminated, the
water blue and frothy, and I wondered where it
all came from, what had borne it, and what force
had guided it to this point where it crashed and
fell over the edge, roaring like a hundred freight
trains.

"Look," I said, pointing to the water below
where it looked to me like the electric lights were
submerged under the darkening waters and she
turned and saw it too and wondered how they
had gotten there.

It overtook us, the force of it, and I placed my
hands on her breasts and felt the tips of them go
hard between my fingers as she moved against
me and lowered her dress.

"Henry," she said, the power of the water is
drawing us together, unable to resist it.

We made love there on the veranda, the
great roar of the falls in our ears, the thrum of

its power vibrating through us as she gave herself to me freely and recklessly in a way she never had before. And for a time I felt as though I had drawn her heart back from the grave where Charlie held it in his cold gray hands all those days and weeks and months. Her passion was a fire in me, burning, burning, until my soul was consumed and the falling water washed away my sins. Afterward we lay there, our skin damp from the mist, our hair wet and tangled, and slept until the night gave way to our destiny.

Garrett rides a pale horse stalking,
the bones and eyes of me in his pockets,
a dusty trail of lies spilling from eyes of deceit,
watching everything around and near him,
his fear coiled like a snake near his feet ready to
strike him down.

Celsa was there and wept that day as though it was really me. And so did Paulina and Rosita and all the rest of the girls I knew and loved in Fort Sumner. Years after they would grow old knowing that it was not me Garrett had murdered (by his own confession) and dropped down deep in a hole with Charlie and Tom where we awaited the Rio Pecos to come and take us.

Manuella was not the best lover I ever had, but that night on the veranda, and in that moment, she was. And I knew in that waning moment she would never be like that with me again. That *we* would never be like that again. In that one moment she was as a drop of rain upon my tongue, and I a man thirsting.

40

IN SMOKE AND BLOOD AND UNCOUNTED TEARS I LOST MY WAY.
— FROM THE JOURNAL OF HENRY MCCARTY

It was there on the veranda overlooking Niagara Falls that I admit, I gave myself completely to Henry for the first time. It was there that I lost my sense of Charlie and knew that I'd taken a passage not just of miles from the New Mexican sand hills, but of time and purpose. The sound of the roaring water had an effect on us, one I cannot explain except to say it made me think of my mother and her untold lovers when Henry reached out and touched my breasts and looked into my eyes.

My shame and guilt seemed washed away and I gave myself to him feeling like petals under soft rain. He spoke my name and drew me close, then lowered my dress and let it fall at my feet and stood there looking at me for the longest time. I was shameless in wanting his attention. This is my confession to God, and all who would read it.

I understood in that long full moment what

my mother did not tell me about the difference between lovers and husbands.

I read what he had to say and feel the dark bitter blood in my heart. How he was sorry that he came and took me away with him, but worse, how he thinks of me as an obligation. I would rather have become a whore selling myself to men in El Paso than to have journeyed through life with a man who thought of me as an obligation.

Had I known that night how he felt I would have taken the small pistol he kept in the pocket of his coat and killed us both and let the waters of fate rush over us and crash us to the sea.

But I did not know it then, and so I gave myself to Henry there on the balcony of a hotel room overlooking the Niagara Falls. Henry told me to hold out my tongue and I did. He said, "Taste the rain," and I did.

The rain tasted as warm and thick as blood and maybe it was.

Maybe it was the beginning of our dying — a long journey home again.

We slept naked throughout the night in each other's arms, there on the balcony above the falls, like Adam and Eve fallen in the garden, struck down, having tasted the fruit of desire. We, the forbidden, asleep in the garden that wasn't our own.

Now he sleeps on the porch in a rocker where

the sun is the warmest. An old man with a wattle and shiny scalp through the sparse sandy hair, and me, a woman who never loved him but who gave herself to him out of passion and revenge.

Passion and revenge.

Someday it will be over for us.

Our sin.

Our passion and revenge.

Sleep, dear Henry, the sleep of the dead, the sleep of Charlie and Tom and all the others whose blood you've known.

Let the Rio Pecos sing your song, sing your song.

Let angels mend your wings, or the sun melt them.

Garrett's dead.

Garrett's dead.

Henry, come see the wound in my heart where you have rent it with your sharp words of love and hate, words scratched in a book and bleeding.

41

**EVERYWHERE I TURN THERE IS TROUBLE
AND EVERYONE IS A POTENTIAL ENEMY,
EVEN OLD FRIENDS FROM THE GRAVE.
— FROM THE JOURNAL OF HENRY McCARTY**

She's been in my room again. I can tell by the
faint smell of cigarette smoke left behind.
Thinks I don't know that she comes in and
snoops around when I'm not here or sleeping on
the porch to the hum of traffic up and down the
street, to the laughter of children, to the chatter
of quarrelsome jays. But I know and I don't
much give a damn. Maybe I owe it to her that she
learn my truths, a little at a time. Maybe that's
why I don't say anything to her, get angry, carry
on like ol' Charlie would have. Charlie was a
good man but had a hell of a temper. He was
crazy jealous of her.

One day he saw me looking at her when we
were all three planting a garden. Tom was there
too, but he was busy teaching his dog a new
trick. He would aim his finger at it and say,
"Pop!" — like a gun going off — and the dog

would roll over and play dead. Every time Tom shot his dog he would laugh and laugh. I was planting beans and Charlie and Manuella were planting onions. We could smell the Rio Feliz on the shifting wind. Made you want to go fishing or for a swim. I don't know why I allowed myself to get caught staring at her, maybe I just stopped caring whether Charlie noticed or not. It was like a game with me, seeing if I could catch her eye, trying to say things to her with my eyes so she'd know what I was thinking. Quite often she would catch me looking at her and her eyes would say, don't look at me that way, Billy, can't you see I'm a married woman and my husband is standing right there. Don't be crazy and get us into trouble. But sometimes she would catch me looking and it was almost as though she invited it, the attention I was giving her.

Sometimes Charlie was irritable with her and scolded her openly and I saw the way it caused her to flinch when he did. Then at night I would lie on their porch and hear them inside, going at it, and I'd wonder how she stood it, to be scolded so harshly, then open her legs for him. I could sometimes close my eyes and just see them like that — his weight, bearing down on her, thrusting and thrusting into her, the rush of her breath each time, Charlie's grunts and her whispers. I wondered sometimes if she wasn't whispering for him to be a bit more gentle or a bit more quiet, afraid I would hear them and know her heart.

It made me angry sometimes to know what he was doing to her, what she was letting him do to her. The Bible says a woman should cleave to her husband, and a husband should cleave to his wife. That's what I would tell myself lying there in the pale of a moonlit night hearing the distant cries of coyotes and Charlie's grunts — that they were cleaving to each other like a husband and wife should.

Charlie looked up all of a sudden from his onion planting and saw me staring at her and said, "Kid, what the hell you looking at my wife like that for?"

Of course Charlie could never stay mad at me for long.

"I was just seeing how beautiful she was with dew on her cheeks," I said. "You have a beautiful wife, Charlie, and you should be proud that men would want to look at her. Take ol' Hector and that fat wife of his with the black bump on her face. Why I guess nobody would ever look twice at Rita, wouldn't you say? Sure, sure, I can understand how you might be a bit jealous, but if I had a wife as good-looking as Manuella there, I wouldn't mind other fellers looking at her. Better that than a fat wife with a black bump on her face, right?"

He wasn't quite sure what he should say to that. He looked around at her as she stood there waiting to see what he might do — draw his pistol and shoot me, or laugh about it.

"Charlie," I said, "you are a lucky man.

Maybe someday I'll find me a woman as pretty as Manuella and just sit around all day and look at her. I'll let you look too if you want and never say a word about it."

"Well, I guess you are right, Kid. I guess I wouldn't want to have a wife that looked like ol' Hector's. I am a lucky man, now ain't I?" Tom was "popping" his dog and grinning foolishly. "Just don't be looking at her like that when I ain't around."

"You don't have to worry about your best pals," I told him. "Pals don't steal one another's gals, do they, Tom?"

Tom laughed.

"You're a poet, Billy," he said.

Then Charlie started planting his onions again and me the beans.

If Charlie knew then what I was thinking about his wife he would have shot me, or tried.

But maybe down deep he knew someday I'd come and take his woman. Maybe he knows it still, cold and wasted in a grave near the Pecos. Tom too. I sold his dog to Billy Barlow, or did I mention that?

After Niagara Falls we went to Texas and I became a Texas Ranger of all things and for a time we lived in a wood house with flower beds and a tin roof that made the rain sound like shelled peas in a pan. Texas is big and easy to get lost in if you know where to hide. It was there that she had our child. Stillborn. We were to call him Joe, after my brother. But he came out life-less, like the twins that came out of Maria's body, the cord wrapped round its neck like a noose of gut.

"Dead, dead," the doctor said, washing his hands in a pan of water till it turned crimson.

Manuella never cried but simply looked into the small staring eyes of the babe.

"God has taken him," she said. "He must have wanted him more than we did."

Such foolish talk. My sins, I thought, have stained my seed among the rocks and thistles. None will grow or rise up. *Dead, dead.*

Two days later I was shot by a man with a harelip.

42

I GUESS IT IS ALRIGHT TO TALK TO THE DEAD AS LONG AS YOU DON'T TRY LIVING WITH THEM.
— FROM THE JOURNAL OF HENRY MCCARTY

I wrote to Mother once years later, after Father died, and told her about the child, how it came with the cord around its neck and I knew when it did not cry as the doctor took it from me that it was dead. I knew that she would want to know about her grandchild. She wrote me back and said this:

I think it must be the sins I've committed with my lovers that has cursed you. The lines of blue ink were splattered in places by her dried tears.

Then a cousin wrote two weeks later and said that my mother had died. The cousin wrote, "I think it was of heartbreak."

Henry was shot by a man with a harelip in the saloon in Del Rio. The bullet entered under his arm and passed out through a rib and for weeks and weeks the wound seeped pus and I thought he might die and that I would have to bury him next to his son, the child I had named Jesus (not Joe as he had wanted) after the Savior.

For days I walked alone along the Rio Grande — the same river along which Henry had walked with the tall white woman in El Paso — and several times thought about throwing myself into its brown waters. There are worse things, I felt, than a quick and passionless death.

Henry coughed blood into a pan and cursed the man who shot him.

I wept in silence over the losses of my life. Not yet thirty years old and so many losses.

This is when Charlie came to visit me the first time.

Henry was coughing behind a closed door and I was sitting at the table drinking coffee and smoking a cigarette, something I'd learned to do watching Henry. I found that I liked tobacco and sugared coffee together.

I was sitting there in the gloaming light near evening, trying hard not to think of Mother's words or of the Savior Child, when Charlie appeared suddenly across from me — sitting there erect in a chair, his back straight, his hair combed neatly. He had such a peaceful look about him, his eyes as soft and sweet as the first day we met when he told me he was going to ask my father if he could marry me.

"I don't mind you went with the Kid," he said. "I always knew he had his eye on you."

I wasn't afraid.

"Dead's not so bad," he said. "Not as bad as you would think."

I asked him if he missed me.

"Yes, terribly," he said. "That's the worst part."

I told him I missed him too. That seemed to please him.

"Well, someday we will be together again," he said. "But now is not the time. I know you walk near the river and have thought about drowning yourself. I've watched you and read your thoughts. The dead have certain powers."

"I could be with you again," I said, "if I were to throw myself into the river."

"It's not the same if you take your *own* life," he said.

I asked him about that but he wouldn't say anything more about it.

"I see you have taken up smoking," he said.

I told him I had changed in many ways.

"Yes, I know. It's okay," he said.

I turned my eyes away for a moment when Henry's cough startled me and when I turned back, Charlie was gone, the room empty and silent and filled with darkness.

The next time I walked by the river I felt no urge to throw myself in. In fact the thought of it now frightened me.

One time Henry said to me, "Who is it that I hear you talking to late at night?"

I told him I was only talking to myself.

He joked and said it was all right as long as I didn't start answering myself. Charlie visited me many times at first, then didn't appear to me again until Henry had gone off to war in Cuba and I met a man named Miller who offered me, among other things, a life of wealth and comfort.

43

**IT DOESN'T MATTER HOW WE SUFFERED
SO MUCH AS HOW WE SURVIVED.
— FROM THE JOURNAL OF HENRY MCCARTY**

"**Why** are you here?" she said.

"Manifest Destiny," I said.

"What is that?"

"I'm not sure," I said, "but it is why I'm here, that's why we are all here."

Her apartment looked out over the sea of blue-green waters.

Her name was Mariel. She said she sold herself to stay alive, to feed her and her child — a young boy who slept on the floor in the corner of the room, curled up like a small brown cat.

"You are much older than most of the soldiers," she said, as she sat on the bed next to me and helped me unbutton my tunic.

"I joined the army late," I said. "Colonel Roosevelt raised this force of volunteers to come fight with him here in Cuba and put down the Spaniards and I saw something about it in the newspaper and joined up. It was just a whim with me at first, though I'd been thinking about it right along — how the Spaniards have committed atrocities against your people. Everybody in my country has heard how they butcher the people down here."

"Si," she said, her fingers undoing the buttons of my jacket.

"And this?" she said, touching a hand to my face where a bullet had grazed my cheek as we charged up Kettle Hill. "You have shed your blood for us."

"Good thing those Spaniards weren't real sharpshooters," I said, "or I might have shed a lot more of it than I did."

"You smile in the face of death."

"Well, if you've been killed as many times as I have, you'd smile too."

She didn't understand and I didn't try to explain it. Others were waiting to get their turn with her. She removed my tunic and folded it neatly and then unlaced my boots and pulled them off, the air in the room was warm and stagnant as I watched the blue-green sea kissing against the white sands of the shoreline through the window of her small room and thought how tragically beautiful it all seemed: the war, the Cuban people in their misery, the sleeping boy.

She stood and removed her dress, her skin the color of copper, her hair black and straight, her breasts swollen, the nipples dark as plums. I placed my hands on her hips and drew her close to me thinking that it had been a long time since

I'd had a woman other than Manuella, thinking how I missed it — having different women — and how far away from everything familiar to me I was.

"Is this part of your Manifest Destiny?" she said, letting me draw her close. "This why you Americanos come here, to liberate our people?"

"If you want to think of it that way."

"I am going to be liberated, eh?"

Her laughter was like strings of a guitar being strummed sadly.

"Yes, liberated," I said. "That's what I'm going to do to you — liberate you from the Spaniards."

"Then I am ready, my soldier man."

Afterward, even though I knew there were others waiting to be with her, I lay on the bed next to her and smoked a cigarette. She asked me if she could smoke one too, and I gave her one.

"Americans make such good cigarettes," she said.

"You will leave soon, now that the war is over?" She blew rings of smoke that drifted to the ceiling.

"Yes, all of us. Then what will you do when the American soldiers are gone?"

She shrugged.

"The same thing, nothing will change for me. Men are all the same no matter which country they are from. The Spanish, the Cubans, the Americanos, they all want the same thing. There will always be men willing to pay me for the pleasure I can give them until I grow too old and ugly. And even then, there are men who will pay me, but less so."

"The boy," I said, indicating the child asleep in the corner. "Where is his father?"

"Dead," she said. "Tortured and murdered by the Butcher Weyler."

"Who's that?"

"The general that Spain sent to oppress our people," she said. "His soldiers came one day and took my husband and I never saw him again. I heard later through the insurrectos that Weyler had my husband hung upside down by his heels and ran hot pokers into his eyes, and when he would not tell them anything, they cut off his penis before Weyler himself shot my husband in the back of his head."

"Why your husband?" I said.

"Because they thought he was one of the insurrectos."

"But he wasn't?"

"Yes, he was." She looked at the boy.

"His name is Jorge, after his father."

"He is lucky to still have you," I said.

"Do you think a child is lucky to have a dead father and a whore for a mother?"

"You shouldn't think of it that way."

"I don't know how else *to* think of it," she said.

"The sea looks inviting. Have you ever swum in it?"

She looked toward the blue-green water as she

256

got up from the bed and began washing herself in preparation for the next man, a wet cloth between her legs and over her limbs.

"Yes, my husband and I used to swim there all the time."

Someone knocked on the door and a rough voice said in English, "Hey, hurry up in there, Henry, some of us fellers would like a turn too!" It sounded like the banker, Fritz, who had charged up Kettle Hill next to me and had a piece of his ear shot away by a Spaniard's bullet and a gold watch with a picture of his wife in the lid.

"You had better go," she said. "They grow inpatient waiting and I must earn what I can while the business is good."

"You are very beautiful," I said.

"When a man has a big need for a woman he will say almost anything, won't he?"

I left her an extra dollar and told her it was for Jorge, the boy who slept while I had sex with his mother in a small room that overlooked the sea.

Mariel. I came across her name in my book just last week when it was raining and I had nothing to do but sit in my room and read what I'd written over these last years. When I came to her name I had to stop and remember for a moment before recalling that time in Cuba when I'd gone down there with Teddy Roosevelt's Rough Riders and we, who had no horses to ride, charged up the hill on foot, the bullets seeking us out. Such was our Manifest Destiny.

A young man named Fred who was from New York and wanted to be an actor was shot in the face and died along with many others. And this was his Manifest Destiny.

I read her name and wondered if she was long since dead, the boy grown, an old man now whose limbs still ache from sleeping on a cold floor in the corner of the room while his mother had sex with soldiers for money and revenge.

Mariel, whose last name I never knew.

I count the names of women in my book and there are twenty-four.

She is one of them.

44

STOLEN FRUIT IS ALWAYS THE SWEETEST. AND WHAT I'VE EATEN, I'VE NOT REGRETTED.
— FROM THE JOURNAL OF HENRY MCCARTY

Henry saw a story in the newspaper and said, "Look here, Colonel Roosevelt's raising an army of volunteers to go fight the Spaniards in Cuba. Says here, it's to be a calvary unit. Why that's just my thing."

"Who is Colonel Roosevelt and where is Cuba?" I asked.

Henry looked at me over the top of the newspaper.

"Does it matter?"

"I thought you loved the Spanish people," I said. "Why would you want to go and fight them?"

He was, by my guess, nearly forty years old, heavier now that he hadn't been shot or on the run for several years and was eating as well as ever.

"It says here it is our duty to fight the Spaniards — they have blown up a warship, the *Maine*, and killed some of our people. President McKinley says we ought to go and fight them, says it's our Manifest Destiny."

"I would think by now that you would be weary of war and getting shot at."

He folded his paper neatly and said, "The only thing that I am weary of is the boredom."

He had been working as a Pinkerton agent in Albany, New York, where we lived in a small house with large chestnut trees lining the streets.

"I think I will go and join up," he said, "and fight those Spaniards."

And that is what he did.

I took work at a shoe factory to support Henry's behavior, after he quit the Pinkertons to join Colonel Roosevelt's army. There was no money with which to live or pay the rent. It didn't seem to matter to him. What mattered to him was his own destiny, not that of President McKinley.

Mr. Miller owned the shoe factory and saw me among the other girls who had gone there to work and came over to where I stood at my stitching machine.

"You are too pretty to work so hard," he said.

He wore a pink carnation in the lapel of his gray suit and his hair was wet and slicked down with rose water and his cheeks and chin were a dark blue where he shaved.

"My husband is off in Cuba fighting the

Spaniards," I said.

"I see," he said. "So you are alone for now."

"Yes."

When I left the shoe factory that late afternoon, Mr. Miller was waiting for me in a new horseless carriage that had horsehair seats and ran on gasoline. He had changed his clothes and now wore a white linen suit and straw boater. These, along with his thin moustaches, made him look very elegant and handsome.

"Please," he said, stepping out to open the door for me. "I'd like for you to go for a ride with me."

"I'm married," I said. "Did I forget to mention that?"

"Yes, I know, you told me earlier, but it is only a ride."

It was quite a thrill and everyone stopped and watched as we drove down the streets of Albany — there were very few of those machines in Albany at the time. We stopped at a restaurant and he asked me if I was hungry.

"You look like you could eat," he said. "This place has the best food in town. Why they even have an oyster bar."

I watched him eat oysters and even tried one myself because he insisted but I didn't care for it all that much.

"Order anything you like," he said. "Everything is good."

I thought about Henry off in Cuba, perhaps shot or killed, lying dead while I ate expensive food with a man who was rich and generous. *You only have yourself to blame,* I thought. *You had no reason to go away and leave me to the fortunes of other men.* The champagne Mr. Miller ordered affected my head.

Later we stopped for ice cream and he drove me home and asked if he could come in and I told him, no, I didn't think it was a good idea and he smiled and said, "Of course, you are a married woman with a husband off fighting a war, how would it look."

Every day after that he would come around and sometimes bring me a fresh flower or a box of candies and the other women giggled and talked behind my back except for Eugenia, whom I had made friends with. Her husband had gone to Florida and a few weeks later wrote her that he had met someone and simply wasn't coming back. She said at first she was stricken to tears, but soon realized that it was foolish to weep for a man with no more loyalty than a tomcat. She laughed when she told me this.

"They say he is very rich and very good in bed," she said about Miller. "I am envious, Manuella, I wish it were me he was bringing candy and flowers to. I'd give him anything he wanted." I asked innocently how she knew this about Mr. Miller and she laughed and said that he was always asking out the prettiest girls who came to work for him.

I thought of my mother and her many lovers and wondered if I was destined to end up taking my life someday, the bitterness of my sins too much to bear.

Mr. Miller and I went to dinner many times together and often he would try and hold my hand or caress my fingers and tell me how beautiful I was. I thought of Henry. What if he were with someone in Cuba, a woman. It wouldn't be unreasonable to think that he was. Henry was very attracted to women and they to him. What if he found someone there and didn't come back like Eugenia's husband? Was I being foolish to reject the proposals that had come increasingly from Mr. Miller? These questions I asked myself each night when he dropped me off in front of the house after asking if he could come in for a nightcap; each time I refused him, but each time my resolve and resistence grew weaker.

And in those lonely moments and hours of lying in my bed, my hands exploring my body, I wondered if I was doing the right thing by spurning Mr. Miller's company. After all, I didn't really love Henry, I reasoned with myself. Sometimes I even loathed him. So why not accept Mr. Miller's advances? The questions were like bees in my head at times, and my own touch wasn't the same as that of a man.

"Look," he said one evening while we were having a supper of roasted pheasant and champagne. "This husband of yours, suppose he is dead or doesn't return for some reason, then what will you do?"

"If he had been killed, I would have heard it by

now. And why wouldn't he return if he is still alive?" I said, but silently thinking of Eugenia's husband.

Mr. Miller bunched his shoulders.

"Why do you suppose he left you in the first place if he loved you so much?"

"He felt it was his duty to go," I said. "He said Colonel Roosevelt would have the Spaniards whipped in no time and that he would probably be back in two weeks."

"No man who loves his wife would voluntarily go off and fight a war of so little significance," Mr. Miller said. "Manuella, I don't think your husband loves you very much."

"And you do?"

This seemed to surprise him and he sat back and stared at me for a long moment, his hand on his glass of champagne.

"You are bold," he said, "I like that in a woman."

"I am not so bold. I simply want to know what we are talking about."

"Yes, yes," he said, smiling because my boldness pleased him.

"I could make your life very comfortable, Manuella. I could put you up to live in a nice place and give you nice clothes to wear, and plenty of money for whatever you wanted. You wouldn't have to work in the shoe factory any longer and wear yourself thin from hard labor."

He reached his hand across the table and took my fingers. I didn't pull away this time.

"You have done this for other girls?"

He looked startled.

"No, never." But his protest came out weak and I didn't believe him.

"Are you saying that you would want to marry me?"

"Marry you?" This too startled him. Then he smiled broadly.

"No, I could not marry you, my sweet. I am already married and so are you."

"So I would be your whore, is that it?"

This time he looked around to see who might be listening.

He shook his head as though disappointed in me, as though he'd asked me a question to which I'd given the wrong answer.

"No, no, of course not — that's a terrible term to use," he said. "Please, perhaps we should talk about this as I take you home."

"If I am not to be your wife and not to be your whore," I said, "then what am I to be?"

He called for the waiter and when he came Mr. Miller handed him some money, then stood, indicating that we were to leave.

"To answer your question," he said, once we were in his horseless carriage, "you would be my special friend, someone I could talk to and unburden myself to when the need arose. You don't know how difficult life can be when you have money and all the responsibility that goes with it. You may think that having money is the answer to all your problems, but it isn't."

"So I would be a friend who would also be willing to listen to you and go to bed with you," I said.

"I'd like to think of it more as sharing yourself with me and me with you. But it wouldn't have to be every time. Sometimes we could just talk and I could tell you my problems."

"Do you think I am that wise," I said, "to give you advice?"

"Yes, of course. Sometimes all it takes is for someone willing to listen."

The carriage chugged along loudly.

"Listen," he said, as he pulled to the side of the road. "I could make sure that you wouldn't ever have to worry about money again. I could set you up an account at the bank and put money into it each month and whenever your husband came back from Cuba, or whenever you decided that you didn't want to be my friend any longer, you could just take whatever is there and do whatever you wanted with it. I wouldn't make it hard for you."

He touched my shoulder, his eyes pleading like those of a little boy who wanted something very desperately.

"Can I kiss you, Manuella?"

I didn't say anything but allowed him to kiss me. His lips were dry and the kiss was nothing really, not for me it wasn't.

Then he pressed himself against me, put his arms around me and held me tightly and whispered my name repeatedly. I stayed stiff in his arms. Afraid to breathe.

Finally he said, "Will you at least consider it?"

I told him I would and he seemed very happy and took me home without asking to come in for a late drink. The next day he appeared at my stitching machine with a box of candy and told me not to open it until I got home and when I did I found a gold bracelet inside and a note that read, "Have you made a decision yet?"

I thought of Charlie and the poor unsuccessful life we'd had together, how my father had sold me to him in the first place, and it was as though that was all the money Charlie had ever been able to accumulate in his short life. I recalled how he wanted to sell a horse one spring to buy me a dress but the horse was so poorly it died before he could. And afterward how endlessly Charlie talked of someday buying me that dress. Then I thought of Henry, who was hardly any more successful than Charlie, for he spent money as fast as he earned it and never gave it any consideration beyond that. I thought of the lovers my mother had and wondered if any of them had been rich and offered her the same thing Mr. Miller was offering me — an "easy life," as he put it.

What if Henry did not return from Cuba? What if he were killed or turned out like Eugenia's husband and abandoned me? I felt more alone and desperate than I'd ever been.

New York and New Mexico were worlds apart. I wanted to someday be able to afford to go home again, to visit my mother's grave and Charlie's and that of my baby son, Jesus. I wanted to smell the sage and juniper — to be again a young woman untouched by sorrow and unsuccessful men.

Eventually, after not hearing from Henry, I consented to let Mr. Miller come in for what he called a "nightcap," and when he lingered and asked if he could kiss me again, I let him; and this time his mouth was warm, his lips soft, and his eagerness transcended into me. His embrace was passionate and it had been ever so long since a man had held me in that way, since I'd had anyone desire me so hungrily. So when Mr. Miller asked if he could lie on the bed with me, I didn't tell him that he should leave.

Afterward, long into the night, he rose from the bed and dressed quickly and said that he was sorry but that he had to go home to his wife and children. I understood and was relieved that he was going.

"You see," he said, as he put on his coat, "it wasn't so bad, was it?"

But it was, I just didn't tell him.

"I want to give you some money," he said. "For the rent, until we can find you something better, something larger. You must feel very closed in here in this small apartment."

The next day a letter arrived from Henry saying that he was on his way home, that the Spaniards "had been whipped." I told this to Mr. Miller when he saw me at the factory the following Monday. "Oh," he said and looked down at his shoes.

"Then you understand that I can't continue to see you or accept your offer."

He fidgeted.

"Well, I suppose if that's the way it is, that's the way it is," he said. "How soon will he arrive? Perhaps we could have dinner tonight one last time, and a nightcap."

I handed him back his money and told him I wasn't a whore and his face flushed red.

"I never meant . . ."

"It's okay," I told him. "I was lonely, I didn't do it for the money."

Now, these years later, I read the name *Mariel* in Henry's book and I do not feel so bad about Mr. Miller, knowing that while I was with him, Henry was with her, a Cuban whore of whom he wrote:

A boy slept on the floor while I took her. She said it was her son, a child whose father had been murdered by the Spaniards. As a woman, she said, she could survive and provide a life for her and the boy. As a woman of God, she could only suffer and that is why she did what she did instead of begging in the streets with a cross around her neck and asking for mercy from a God who had put her in such a position in the first place. She said that the war was not such a terrible thing, for it brought her plenty of business, and that the soldiers paid better than the local men and were kinder to her. She said many of the soldiers had proposed marriage to her but she never took them seriously because they had wives and girlfriends they would go home to after the war was over and forget all about her. She liked American soldiers the best, she said. I asked her if she'd ever slept with any of the Spaniards before the war began and she admitted that she had because their money was as good as anyone else's. These were perhaps some of the same ones who had killed her husband. She was a very brave and honest woman who understood that vengeance would do nothing for the sleeping child. Because of these things, I write her name in my book. Like Tunstall and Charlie and Tom, Mariel had a good heart and gave me what I needed. I think I loved her for bravery.

Mr. Miller was killed by a train that struck his horseless carriage when it stalled on the railroad tracks. He was with a young woman from the factory who was also killed. They said she was very beautiful and was pregnant with his child. But can you understand now why Mr. Miller is my one secret that I have kept from Henry all these years?

BOOK THREE

45

HELL, ALL I KNOW IS, YOU SHOOT FIRST, OR YOU DON'T.
— FROM THE JOURNAL OF HENRY MCCARTY

Horse's hide dark wet from rain, standing in a field of alfalfa. Nostrils snuffling, ears pricked. Rain falls upon the just and unjust alike. We live our lives differently but death treats us fair and square. Rich man, poor man, sinner, saint.

On a dreary day in September I saw a horse standing in a field of alfalfa alone, its hide dark wet from the rain, and it caused me to think of how much I missed the Wild West, New Mexico and Texas and the Rio Grande — the bloody land that swallowed our souls and gave us back nothing. But still, I missed it, and so did Manuella.

She said, "I'd like to go home for a visit and see where Mother is buried."

"You know," I said, "we do that and anyone hears I'm still kicking, there could be a fuss."

"Oh, Henry," she said. "They all think that

you are dead, dead, dead, and in your grave there beyond the wall close by the Pecos River with Charlie and Tom. Why someone has even carved a stone with your names on it."

I said that I would have to consider it, then went for a walk and saw the horse in the alfalfa field, standing alone as though waiting for its rider to come. I stood there in the rain and whistled and it flicked its ears and turned its head and looked my way. Been years since I rode a horse. They have carriages now with gasoline engines, and trolley cars. In Albany you don't see many men ride horses. I whistled again and the filly came through the mist up to the fence and let me stroke her neck, snuffling my hands with her black soft nose for an apple or carrot.

"I could ride you all the way to Lincoln," I said. "Two thousand miles and we'd be there and wouldn't Garrett shit a brick." This is a term I picked up in Cuba among the soldiers and I liked using it very much.

The horse flicked its ears and I could see mesas and mesquite and rolling hills in those large dark eyes. An alfalfa field in Albany, New York, was no place for a good horse.

"Mother had lovers," Manuella said to me one night when I was still thinking of the horse. There was no moon and it was dark as a well. "My father wasn't the only man she knew."

"Did she tell you about them?" I said.

"No. I never knew until her letter arrived, the

one that said the reason the baby died was because of the sins she'd committed with her lovers."

"If sin was the cause," I said, "it was mine and none of her own."

"She died of heartbreak because she blamed herself for the death of Jesus."

"*Jesus?*"

"Yes, it is what I called him in my heart," she said. "Jesus."

"You've changed while I was gone away to war. You are different now, Manuella."

And for the first time since I'd returned, she looked at me without flinching.

"We all change," she said. "Your going away had nothing to do with it."

I bought two tickets on the Southern Pacific that would take us to Santa Fe and bought her a new dress, thinking of the one Charlie could never afford, thinking that if I took her home again in a new dress somehow it might get better between us.

We rode the train, the hum of steel rails
coming up through our feet and into our bones
Steel rails, steel rails, carrying us home,
carrying us home.
To the abandoned places we return.

46

**THE FLOODS OF MEMORIES PAST RISE UP TO
DROWN US IF WE AREN'T VIGILANT.
— FROM THE JOURNAL OF HENRY MCCARTY**

Henry looked hopeful going home again. His reflection in the window of the Pullman while a
porter took tickets and a candy butcher sold taffy
seemed an image born of water. Seeing his fea-
tures in the rain-stained glass was like looking at
a ghost beneath a watery grave.

"Didn't realize how far we'd come," he said at
one point when we saw tall corn growing row
upon row as far as the horizon. It was in Indiana,
I think. The green tongues of cornstalks lapped
the rain.

The trip took six days in all and Henry said he
could feel the train wheels vibrating in his blood
when we stepped onto the station platform in
Santa Fe.

"Met Jesse James here once, and his brother
Frank," Henry said. "They came here looking
for new banks to rob and figured the pickings
were easy. I told them they better think again.

Told them Mexican lawmen were bad hombres. Jess was a good-looking man and had a thick dark beard. Frank was taller and more nervous. Now Jess is dead and Frank's going around the country giving lectures about crime not paying. Got a snow-white beard down to here."

We could smell the pinon trees and see the snow-capped Sangre de Christo Mountains stark against a glass blue sky. *The blood of Christ,* I thought, has flowed from the mountains into our veins, bones heaped upon bones make the mountains, our tears make the rivers, our sighs the wind. The land is in us — "ashes to ashes," says the Bible, "and dust to dust." Jesus took a daub of mud and spat into it and rubbed it on a blind man's eyes and he was able to see again. Such is the earth's power. The land hears my song and sings to me of the dead and the living, sings to me of Charlie's bones turning to dust again. Sings to me of fever and blood as I watch Henry buy a cigar and smoke it.

In the plaza Indians sell fried bread and trinkets to the departing passengers, many of whom are from New York and Philadelphia and Chicago. Ladies in bustled skirts and men in beaver bowlers and silk shirts with celluloid collars come west to see the frontier, to see wild Indians and men like Billy the Kid. The Wild West! Do they know the price of admission is blood?

"Goddamn poor bastards," Henry says. "Look what we did to them" — meaning the Indians. "I bet there ain't a Mescalero Apache among the bunch. Too proud to beg the white man's favor. An Apache would just as soon kill you as to ask you for a nickel." He seemed duly upset.

The air is crisp and clean and I am glad to breathe it in once again; the East had a smell like no other place I'd been, and except for the raging water of the Great Falls, I never cared for it much. I was glad to be so far away from it, from the shoe factory and Mr. Miller's dry mouth and damp hands on me.

"I'll hire us a hack," Henry says, "and we'll leave today for Lincoln."

By now he'd grown a heavy beard and wore spectacles because one eye was going dim. And if you looked at him dressed as he was in his brown suit and bowler hat you wouldn't recognize him from the old days. No longer a shaggy-headed youth with pistols strapped to his side, standing in tall boots with his pants tucked in them, standing in front of a box camera a ragged border ruffian. No longer did he smell like wind and horse, or squat on his heels in the dust and squint toward the unknown distance. Henry was a man now, middle-aged and handsome with a serious gaze. I watched him pause before a plate-glass window of a saloon and take stock of himself. He saw what I saw — a man far removed from the past violence of the Lincoln County Wars, which were now barely a single thread of memory tying him to his bloody past.

I noticed too how he patted the bulge in his

right-hand coat pocket, where he kept a small pistol to "keep things even in case I run into Garrett," he said. We'd long since lost all track of Pat Garrett and were not sure if he was alive or dead. Henry had a sense about such matters and didn't believe that Garrett was dead and feared that he might run into him on the street or in a saloon and not be armed.

"If I see him I'll kill him" is how Henry put it.

"I thought you'd gotten over all that nonsense," I would say whenever the subject of Garrett came into our conversation.

He would always look at me in the strangest way.

"I don't forget what's been done to me," he said. "I don't ever forget, and if I see Garrett I'll finish him."

His words were like acid on my skin.

Three days travel by hack found us in Lincoln. The town had not changed, except Murphy and Dolan were gone, gone, gone — as were McSween and Tunstall. Henry pointed to the upper rooms of the old Murphy-Dolan store and said, "From that window I shot Ollinger. He died right there, near that cottonwood, full of dimes."

The street was lazy with people and I held my breath, thinking that someone would recognize us, but no one did. We drove past the Wortley Hotel and the homes of Cisneros, Stanley, and Aguayo, Henry pointing out each one to me, saying how at one time they'd all been friends. We drove past Ike Stockton's old saloon, which was now closed and boarded up, and next to it Montano's store. We drove past the old jail and across from it stood Sheriff Brady's house where now several Mexican children played in the front yard and an old man with nut-brown skin sat on the porch and watched them and watched us as we passed.

Henry's jaw muscle twitched.

We drove east for a time, then south, until we eventually reached the homestead of my childhood near the Rio Penasco.

I was amazed at how small the crumbling adobe looked to me now as a grown woman. Had we really all lived in such confinement? It seemed impossible. I didn't remember it as being cramped, but with four brothers and three sisters and my parents it surely must have been.

"Looks like a good home for rattlers and scorpions," Henry said, helping me down from the carriage. "Why look, the roof has fallen in."

I peered in the windows and through the door where the shadows were darkest and saw nothing but emptiness. There was no trace of the home I once knew, no trace of laughter or tears or of a mother whose wistful gaze saw lovers beyond the cooking pots and ollas. There was no trace of the man who had sold me to Charlie Bowdre.

"Be hard-pressed to stay dry if it rained," Henry said, looking at the collapsed roof.

I felt as though part of me lay under the roof, crushed into the dirt.

Henry smoked a cigarette and walked around kicking at a pile of rusting cans while I pressed my hands against the adobe walls and drew from them the last warmth of the autumn sun.

"It's like everything else," he said. "Gone, gone, gone. Charlie, Tom, you, me, this old place. Gone, blown away, like our dreams." He kicked a tumbleweed and it shattered into brown dust.

We followed the Rio Penasco toward my cousin's house several miles away. She, Juanita, was the one who'd written me that Mother had died of heartbreak. I wanted to visit her and learn where the grave was.

Juanita was old and fat beyond her years, a brood hen with too many chicks. Her husband, Alfredo, was still a slender stick of a man whose eyes never seemed to leave her hips or heavy breasts. An old rooster with startling eyes.

Juanita shook her head and asked twice if I was really Manuella. She looked at Henry suspiciously and I told her that he was a man I'd met in New York, a Mr. Miller. This seemed to satisfy her curiosity.

"There were rumors that El Chivato had returned from the dead and that you had taken up with him," she whispered when Henry paid a visit to the privy and we were alone. "At first I thought that it might be *him*." I assured her that Billy was dead and that the man was not El

Chivato. She blinked with uncertainty, then seemed to accept my explanation.

"When you left this country I thought I would never see you again. Did you get my letter about your mama?" she asked, wiping corn flour from her hands onto a dusty apron.

I asked her where the grave was and she told me that it had been not far from our house but that the river had flooded so often that she wasn't sure anymore.

"Each time the river floods it changes its course a little, and now, after all these years, I can't be certain."

It made me sad to think that my mother's grave, her soul and her bones, might be forever lost. It is the water that carries us to the world of the dead, to the place the living cannot go.

Juanita fixed us a meal and we ate in near silence except for the many children, who seemed fascinated with Henry. He charmed them terribly by making a silver dollar disappear, then pulling it from the ear of this one or that one, causing them to laugh as though he were tickling them.

Alfredo simply watched like an old child himself, a smile on his lips, proud of what he'd bred — his seed alive in their fat brown faces and wriggling bodies.

"You never asked about your father," Juanita said after we'd finished the meal and I was helping her clean the table. "Aren't you curious?"

"I thought about him, yes."

"But you didn't ask."

"I assume that he found a new wife," I said.

"No, no. He never did. After your mama died your papa left for Las Vegas, where they say he gambled and drank heavily. Alfredo and I took in your brothers and sisters and raised them as our own."

"And you never heard from him again?" I said.

"Once. He sent some money for the children and a note that said he was doing well for himself in the cattle business and would send more money each month to help with their care."

"Did he?"

"No," she said, shaking her head. "We never heard from him again."

"My brothers and sisters," I said, "do you know where they are?"

Sadness filled her eyes and she sighed heavily in resignation before telling me bad news.

"Alberto died shortly after your father left for Las Vegas. He was kicked by a horse and that did it. Rosa met a man and went off with him, a gringo cowboy, just as you had done with Charlie. Carmen went to Santa Fe, where I heard later she'd become a prostitute and eventually drank mercury and died. Ricardo and Pepe and Francisco went off to become vaqueros — they worked for a time for Mr. Chisum, then when he died they went either to Texas or Mexico, I'm not sure which."

"Chisum dead?" Henry said, suddenly distracted from his tricks with the children.

"Si. Four years after the cattle wars," Alfredo said.

"And Ysleta?" I asked, wondering why she did not mention my youngest sister's name.

She lowered her eyes.

"Dolan," she said. "Ysleta became Mr. Dolan's sweetheart, his *other* woman."

I didn't understand, though I remembered J. J. Dolan as being a small, sharp-faced man who'd been on the opposing side of Henry and Charlie and Mr. Tunstall in the range wars. I remembered too that he was married to a tall, large-boned woman who wore feathered hats.

"When he would not leave his wife and marry her," Juanita said, "she became drunk on opium and either fell or threw herself into the Rio Bonito and drowned."

There it was, another member of my family taken by water.

Of my sisters, Juanita reported that only one had survived — Rosa, who went away with the white cowboy. I felt more alone and abandoned than I ever had. Henry was smoking cigarettes on the porch and talking in Spanish to Alfredo, asking him if they still spoke of Billy the Kid, and Alfredo saying sure, that there had been many reports of the Kid's existence, that the sheriff, Garrett, did not kill the Kid that night but another man instead, and that the Kid was often seen in the territory still.

I heard Henry's laughter as he expressed his

dismay at such reports.

"Why, everybody knows ol' Pat shot and killed Billy Bonney that night — they even held a coroner's inquest and had a bunch of witnesses sign it."

"No, no," Alfredo said, "it was all a bunch of lies. The people of Fort Sumner agreed to it to protect the Kid and to pacify Garrett."

"Why would they?" Henry said, goading Alfredo to tell his version of the account.

"Because they loved the one but not the other and were frightened of both. Even now, after years and years, they would not tell anyone the truth even though they all know it."

"Do you have any liquor, compadre? I'd like to drink a toast to such a beautiful sunset."

"And to El Chivato?" Alfredo said.

"Si, to El Chivato," Henry said.

That night we slept on one of the children's beds, the children sleeping on the floor like so many lazy cats, their meowing soft, rhythmic like distant wind.

"I've come home for nothing," I said. "My family has suffered the same fate as the old house."

"What did you expect, Manuella? Nothing is what it used to be."

I felt my body floating to the heavens, felt the absence of a soul, as though God had taken it, along with my brothers and sisters, along with my madre and padre. Sometime late in the night

Charlie came and beckoned me to join him outside in the yard and I did.

"I ride the white wind, Manuella," he said, the yard filled with moonlight, his eyes glowing like burning embers.

"I want to ride it too."

"Not yet, not yet. Death is eternal, my darling — don't rush into it."

"Mama, Ysleta, Carmen, Alberto, are they in that place with you?" I said. "Do they ride the white wind?"

But he refused to answer any questions about the dead.

"Don't trouble yourself with such matters," he said. "You will soon enough know the answers."

"Will you be waiting for me, Charlie? Will you come get me when it is time?"

"I will take you over when it is time, this I promise."

I wept and he pointed to a distant star and said, "There," but I didn't know what he meant. Then he was gone, faded into the moonlight, and I felt breathless because he hadn't taken me with him.

The next morning I awakened to a ring of children around my bed, Henry's side empty, and when I asked Juanita if she had seen him, she said, "He saddled one of Alfredo's horses and said that he was going out for a ride and might not be back for one or two days." Then she said, taking my hand in hers, "Your Mr. Miller is quite handsome, Manuella, you are lucky to find two handsome men in the same life. He is even more handsome than Charlie. How do you do it?"

I could only think that Henry had brought me home to leave me, to unburden himself of me, and the feeling wasn't all that terrible in some respects. But in other ways it was.

I searched for three days for my mother's grave and never found it. I prayed she was with her lovers among the stars. That the wild river had swept her to the stars, floated her from earth to the heavens.

47

**SOME DIED BEFORE I COULD KILL THEM,
ROBBING ME OF THE PLEASURE.
— FROM THE JOURNAL OF HENRY MCCARTY**

Soon as I heard that ol' Jug Ears Chisum was dead I knew I had to go have a look for myself. I asked Alfredo to lend me a sound horse and he said he had a piebald mare that stood sixteen hands and could outrun the wind if I wanted her to and I said there wasn't much I liked better than fast horses and saucy women, to which he laughed and passed me his crock of mescal.

Had dreams that night about Garrett; maybe it was all those children sleeping on the floor around the bed mewing like kittens in their sleep that did it. Or maybe it was too much of the mescal and stomping around old territory that did it. Anyway, in the dream Garrett was standing in the doorway of Pete Maxwell's, blood dripping off his hands and a bloody butcher knife in his belt.

"I killed Pete," he said. "Stabbed him and stabbed him."

"Why?" I asked.

" 'Cause he wouldn't tell me where you were, Kid."

"I'm right here, Pat. Let's get to it if that's what you have in mind."

Blood dripped from his fingers like a slow, red rain splattering his fancy boots.

"Sure, sure, Kid, I aim to finish you. I'll kill every goddamn man, woman, and child in Fort Sumner if I have to just to get it done."

"I'm waiting, Pat. Pull your piece or get to cutting."

He came at me, slashing with his butcher knife, wild-eyed and tall, grabbed my wrists before I could jerk the Lightning from my holster, had me in his grip, and it was all I could do to hold him off. Knocked me down, knocked me senseless, then stood over me, his bloody knife ready to strike, and I shouted, no! and that's when I woke, breathing hard, Manuella asleep beside me. All around on the floor, the brown bodies of children, moonlight draped over them like a silver Mexican blanket. I knew right then that Garrett was still alive. I got up, stepped over the sleeping form of a girl whose black braids were lying like snakes about her head, and looked out the window, thinking I would see him there, sitting a white horse, waiting for me to come out.

But all I saw was a moonlit yard. Then a single cloud passed in front of the moon and I knew it was Tom or Charlie or someone dead, but not

Garrett, and not me. I found Alfredo's crock of liquor on the porch where he'd left it and took a long pull from it to settle my thoughts.

Couldn't sleep the rest of the night so didn't try and got up first light, went out to the mesquite corral, and picked out the tall, piebald mare Alfredo said could outrun the wind. Wondered if she could outrun a ghost.

Didn't bother to wake Manuella or anyone else. Simply threw a saddle on the leggy horse and headed toward South Springs near Roswell where John Chisum's ranch was located, thinking it might be all tumbleweeds now, the roof caved in like it had been at Manuella's old place. Thinking that if I got there and found John I'd kill him. Never hated the man, just never did know who he was bringing to the dance — Murphy or Tunstall. And if he was already dead, like Alfredo said, I'd piss on his grave and give a shout. Something about coming back to this mystical land had stirred up all my old passions, and some new ones too. Thought it wouldn't, but it did. Some might see it as a blood feud. I just saw it as finishing the job somebody else had begun. If they had left me out of it I would have stayed out, but that wasn't possible. And now there were still the dead that needed avenging, cries from the graves for justice. I thought, were it me, I'd not want somebody to just walk away from it, forget I'd given my blood and bones to a war that meant nothing in the end. But then, I guess you look at it in a certain way, ain't that what all wars are anyway? Just worthless causes. Don't matter though once you've spilled your blood, spilled the blood of others — it needs finishing. That's the way I looked at it then, that's the way I look at it now. I don't regret what I done. Least most of it I don't.

Alfredo was right about the mare. I let her have her head and she ran so swift I lost my hat and had to turn around and go back and pick it off a prickly pear and pull out the thorns before I could set it on my head again. Riding fast like that reminded me of the races I used to win over near Ruidoso. Won a hundred and eighty dollars in one day racing horses there.

Late afternoon found me at Chisum's ranch near the confluence of the Rio Hondo and the Pecos. It was a long, low-slung affair surrounded by orchards, gardens, and a white picket fence. I noticed the orchards and gardens seemed in good repair and took the pistol from my coat and placed it in the waistband of my trousers over my left hip bone. If ol' John wasn't alive to prune his apple trees, someone sure the hell was.

I drew up to a water tank and dismounted and let the mare drink her fill, noticed the way the water drops fell from her muzzle like diamonds in the sunlight. A horse can be a beautiful creature.

Still no sign of life. It was like someone had been there but left the minute they saw me coming. I tied the mare off at the gate of the picket fence and took the Lightning from my waistband before knocking on the front door.

No answer.

Knock again.

No answer.

Hell's bells.

Then I heard a voice from behind me say, "What you want?"

I quick turned around, aiming my piece at whoever was behind the voice, and saw an old black man, with a horseshoe of hair like cotton batting, hatless in the sun, a hoe in his hands.

I knew who he was, even though it'd been years since I rode up and sat with ol' Jug Ears and Sallie — John having him demonstrate how he could hit a target a half-mile off. His way of warning me not to steal his cattle.

"Came to see John Chisum," I said.

"You're too late you want to speak to him," said Abe Lincoln Washington. For that was his name if I remembered correctly, even though back in those days everyone referred to him as "Chisum's nigger."

"Mr. John is dead," he said. "Died a long time ago."

"You remember me?" I said.

He looked at me for several seconds, then said, "Yes, suh. I remember you, all right."

"How come if Chisum's dead you're still here?"

"Got to be someplace, here's as good as any. Miss Sallie said I could stay on for as long as I wanted. She's gone too."

"Dead, you mean?"

He shook his head.

"No, suh, married and gone is what I meant."

"You still shooting cow thieves?" I said.

He wiped his forehead with the cuff of his right sleeve. His shirt was blue and faded and frayed at the cuffs.

"No, suh, ain't shot nobody in a long time, not since Mister John passed on."

"Why not?"

"Got no reason to. I only did it 'cause that was my job whilst he was alive. Now I tend the apples and apricots, hoe the weeds out'n the lettuce and carrot rows. Tend my strawberries."

"You like that sort of work?" I said.

"Likes it well enough."

"You ever kill any friends of mine?"

"Might have, yes, suh, if they was stealing Mr. John's cows."

He saw the pistol in my hand. Fact was, he hardly took his gaze from it except to wipe his brow that one time.

"You intending on shooting me?" he said.

"Hell no," I said, and put the pistol in my pocket.

"Well, suh, then I guess I best get on back to hoeing them weeds — they sho don't hoe theyselves."

"How'd Chisum die?" I asked.

He turned slightly, looked off toward the orchards.

"In his sleep," he said. "Jus' went to sleep

and never woke up."

He turned to go back to his gardens.

"Mister Washington," I said. "Anybody ask, you never saw me."

He didn't turn around this time but said over his shoulder, "No, suh, I ain't never seen you, Mr. Bonney. Far as I'm concerned, you as dead as ol' Mr. John."

Died in his *sleep*.

John Chisum was one of the luckiest sons of bitches I ever knew in life or death.

48

**THE LITTLE DEATHS WE SUFFER EVERY DAY
MAKE LIFE A LOT HARDER THAN IT SHOULD
BE. TELL ME, WHERE IS GOD IN ALL THIS?
— FROM THE JOURNAL OF HENRY McCARTY**

Henry came back in three days and said, "John Chisum's dead for sure, just like Alfredo said he was."

"I thought maybe you'd gone to see Susan McSween," I said, partly to test his loyalty to me. I knew how he felt about her; I'd heard the rumors about her passion for younger men. Charlie had told me that she acted especially fond of Henry when he was in the employment of Mr. Tunstall and later Alexander McSween, her husband. Charlie said the day the soldiers set fire to the McSween house that Henry and Susan played the piano together and sang "Silver Threads Among the Gold" and that it was an inspiring sight. Who but lovers would do such a thing?

"Susan McSween?" he said with puzzlement.

"I didn't know. You left without a word. How

did I know where you'd gone, or why, or if you would ever return?"

"If you don't know anything about me by now," he said, "you never will," and sat down at the table and said he was hungry from a long ride.

"There is nothing left here for either of us," Henry said that evening as we sat on the porch and listened to the buzz of cicadas. "Hell, practically everyone is dead except Garrett, and he's not in the territory."

I told him I didn't want to go back to New York and he said, "Hell, me either."

We sat for a time, each with our own thoughts about the future, the way people will do who aren't exactly in love and yet not exactly free to go their separate ways.

"Mesilla's pretty," he said. "They have a nice plaza there and dances every Saturday night."

"So is Santa Fe," I said, "and there is more opportunity."

"Opportunity for what?" he said.

"You think Garrett is in Mesilla," I said. "That is why you are interested in going there."

He laughed and told me I was being foolish.

"Why would I want to go live in a place Pat Garrett is hanging out in?" he said.

"You want to find him and kill him."

"Now you are being foolish."

"Tell me you wouldn't if you had the chance."

He rubbed his side, the one that was constantly troubling him, where the man with the harelip had shot him.

"Might rain," he said. "I can always tell when it's going to rain. Parts of me start to ache."

"Garrett might kill you again if he sees you first," I said.

He winced at such a pronouncement.

"He never killed me the first time."

"He wrote a book about it — everyone thinks he killed you."

"He won't be writing any more books, Pat Garrett won't." He ground his teeth as he said it.

"It's been almost twenty years since he shot you dead, dead, dead, in old Fort Sumner."

He rubbed his hands together and examined them as though they held some of the pain he'd removed from his side where the bullet had come out. The wound still wept sometimes.

"You think this Jesus of yours knows a man's sins?" he asked.

"Yes."

"You think he metes out punishment and justice according to each man's sins?"

"I don't understand that word." Henry had been reading a lot the last several years and had taken great pride in learning new words and using them in his conversation. This word, *mete*, I didn't understand.

"Means to hand out," he said. "You think this Jesus of yours hands out punishment and justice according to each man's sins?"

"Yes, I do."

"But if he don't?"

"I believe in him, in his fairness and goodness," I said. "You either believe or you don't."

"I don't," he said. "Seems to me we're put here to take care of our own. How is one man with a world full of people going to worry about a few Mexicans and bandits in a cactus patch like this?"

It angered me for him to question my God in the light of his own ignorance. What did this faithless man know about it?

"God does not turn away, even from the worst sinner," I said.

He scratched a sign in the dirt with the toe of his boot.

"God's the daddy, Jesus the son — that about right? This God let his own boy get hanged on a cross, let him get nails driven into his hands and feet. Let them stick a spear in him, laugh at him. He let him die like the worst kind of criminal," he said. "What you think's going to happen to people like us, he lets his own boy die like that?"

"You are vile for your words," I said, fully ready to leave him, to tell him to leave me. At times he could be so hard and cruel with his words. At times I loved the man who sold me to Charlie Bowdre a hundred times more than I ever could Billy the Kid.

"Maybe so," he said. "But tell me how to make sense of it."

"I'll pray for you."

"Don't bother. It's too late for praying."

We left for Mesilla the next morning, but when we arrived Henry quickly learned that Pat Garrett wasn't there. He spent much of his time over the next several months drinking in the saloons and playing cards and staying out late only to come home restless, to pace the floors at night and stare out the windows.

He hardly ever touched me anymore. And when he did there was no passion in his words, no tenderness in his hands, as there once had been. I could have been anybody, any whore.

"Your hands tell the truth, your words the lies," I said to him one night after he had rolled off of me and went and stood by the window.

"What's that supposed to mean?"

"You treat me as you would a whore, someone you pay money to."

"Christ," he said. "I'd like to find Garrett and kill him."

"Then go and find him and kill him and be done with it."

To this, he turned and stared at me.

"I don't see why you think that I treat you like a whore. You spend too much time on your knees before God, praying to him to trade my life for Charlie's. You don't think I know what you are thinking, what you are praying for? But I know. I know, Manuella. You're as open as any book."

After that night it was a long time before he touched me again and when he did his fingers were as cold as iron and afterward he lay on the bed prostrate like a fallen martyr.

"Garrett never killed me," he said, his lips pressed to the blanket. "He never did."

49

**DON'T VISIT UPON ME YOUR PITY OR YOUR
PLEAS FOR MERCY — I'VE NOTHING LEFT TO
THROW INTO THE HUMAN STEW.
— FROM THE JOURNAL OF HENRY MCCARTY**

This I read in the *Rio Grande Republican* two
days into March that year (this was in 1908):

Pat Garrett, famed lawman and slayer of Billy
the Kid, was himself slain along the Mail-
Scott Road outside of Organ, N.M., by an
unknown assailant or assailants. Conflicting
testimony as to exactly how the former El
Paso tax collector was done in have shrouded
the murder in mystery. A Wayne Brazil, or
Brazil, has been named as a participant in the
crime. Another name that is bandied about is
that of "Killing" Jim Miller — a well-known
Texas gun artist, who is reported to have
been an old adversary of Garrett's, was in the
vicinity at the time. Several are being questioned. The late Mr. Garrett was fifty-eight
years old at the time of his death. He is sur-

vived by a wife and several children. Another good citizen felled by outlawry.

I looked at Henry, who was nearly fifty years old himself, and thought he had finally caught Garrett, no matter what or who the paper said. He was polishing his boots and I dropped the paper on the table, where he could see the article, and said, "You finally took care of him."

He barely paused, stroking the brush over the toe of his boot, the polish like a veil of brown silk across the toe.

"Took care of who?"

"Him," I said. He looked where my finger was pointing, there on the print.

"I don't have my reading glasses, what's it say?"

"I'll go and get them for you so you can read it yourself." And that's what I did and handed them to him and he put them on, slowly and meticulously, as though he were about to read some important legal document. Then, picking up the *Republican*, he read for what seemed to be a very long time before folding it and placing it on the floor to set his freshly polished boots on.

"Somebody finally cooked his hash" is all he said.

"It was you."

He pretended not to hear and walked from the table to the stove and poured himself some coffee, then walked out on the porch in his stocking feet and stood there watching some children playing across the street.

"You didn't have to kill him, Billy."

"I asked that you not call me that. Didn't I ask that of you a long time ago?"

"Slain," I said. "The papers said Garrett was slain and that he was fifty-eight years old and had a wife and children."

"What does any of that have to do with anything? We all die, we all leave people behind to mourn us. Maybe it was just his time."

"It's never a person's time when someone murders him."

He turned then, his eyes as dark as thunderclouds.

"It wasn't Charlie's or Tom's time either. Or have you forgotten, Manuella? It wasn't McSween's or Tunstall's time. It wasn't Brady's or that son of a bitch Ollinger's time. But you know what, in a way it was, because they're all dead, dead, dead. Now Garrett has joined them and who's to say whether it was his time or not? For most surely it was or he wouldn't have died on some dirt road taking a piss on a rock."

I knew then he'd done it. The newspaper said nothing about what Garrett was doing when he was shot.

"You'll pay the devil, Billy." I called him Billy because I wanted him to know how angry I was at him. I didn't mourn Garrett, but did grieve for his wife and children, knowing the emptiness that would be left in their frail hearts.

"You act like Garrett was a friend," he said,

his voice angry, and whenever it got that way he spoke as though he had a mouthful of pebbles. "Hell, anything, you should be dancing with joy."

"Garrett's murder won't bring back Charlie. Of all the people who should know that you should, Billy. You have to let go of the past or you will take it with you to your grave."

"Garrett died a stinking death but I didn't do it."

That was all he would say. Flushed, he went to his room and shut the door and turned the lock. Later I could hear his pen scratching and thought, ink is not blood, Billy, you cannot bleed the poison from your veins by writing words in a book.

I thought of Garrett, of Charlie and Tom, of my mother and brothers and sisters. I thought how time sweeps the earth clean of people like a big broom in the hands of a mad woman who indiscriminately sweeps away the good and the bad alike while leaving the good and the bad in its missed places — like dust under the bed or unseen corners. Sweeps away some so there will be room for others, who will themselves be swept away. We are born of water and end up as dust.

Water and blood cleanse us.
Time descends like dust
The broom sweeps clean.
Broken the dreams like bones,

The good and the un-good are given
Back to the earth — water to mud, mud
  to dust.
I fly, I fly, my eye like a hawk
Searching the river for the lost ones.
These that I loved, and love still
While the walking dead beg my hatred.

The pen ceases its scratch beyond the door
and I hear the creak of bedsprings and soon the
snore of Henry restless in his dreams with no
more fear of Garrett riding a pale horse. And in
the mirror I catch a glimpse of myself, tall and
wan without a trace of beauty left me. I am the
cup from which men drank — Charlie and Mr.
Miller, Garrett and Billy — and did not
replenish.

Damn them all. And damn me for letting them
steal so much.

50

**DEATH, FLY ON PAST MY DOOR, I'M NOT
READY FOR YOU YET.
— FROM THE JOURNAL OF HENRY MCCARTY**

"You've come to kill me," he said.

"It's been a long time, Pat."

"Caught me out here, or did you follow?"

"Followed. Been following you for years, on
and off. Went to New York once, saw Niagara
Falls. You ever been that far east?"

He looked old, hair like graying feathers when
he removed his hat and wiped the sweat from his
brow.

"Surprised you'd ever show your mug in this
country again."

"I'm an all-around surprising fellow, Pat."

"Let it go, Kid. What's past is past. Nobody
cares anymore — what did or didn't happen."

"I care, Pat."

"Shit," he said, and spat, raising a brown
bubble in the dust. "What the fuck you care
about any of that? You're alive, ain't you?"

He wiped the band of his hat with a kerchief

and I could see the way the palsy had took his hands. He saw that I saw and said, "Whiskey, too goddamn much of it. It's ruined my hands, they shake all the time. Couldn't hit a bull's ass with a ten-gauge."

"That why you still carrying one up under your wagon seat?"

He looked over at it. Didn't have to be a mind reader to know he'd have given his nuts to get those palsied hands on it and pull both triggers on me. What had been a lie for him had become the truth. I was dead in his mind and should have stayed that way and now that I wasn't he would have given his nuts to put my name in the obituaries.

"Carry the goddamn thing for snakes. This country's full of snakes."

"I ended up with Charlie's wife. You remember her, Pat, Manuella?"

"Yeah," he said. "I remember she was too good a looking woman for Charlie. How is she, Bill, like what you'd imagined her to be?"

"Living in Mesilla in a two-room apartment over a pharmacy."

He shook his head.

"Probably got kids," he said. "I got four of my own."

"You want that scattergun, Pat, just go ahead and reach over and take it. That's all you have to do."

"I got to take a piss, Kid, *that's* what I got to do. It's why I stopped."

"Hold your water till we're through talking."

He shifted his weight — hard for an old man to hold his water.

"Look, killing me, what's that going to accomplish? You think anybody gives a shit about me or you or any of that business back in Lincoln?"

"Somebody does," I said.

"Who?"

"Me, Pat. I told you I don't ever forget."

"Goddamn, Bill, but I got to piss real bad."

"Go ahead then. Do what you have to do, Pat."

He turned, saying how he didn't think he could go having me watch him like that. Then as he was turning he made a grab for the ten-gauge and that's when I shot him. I think through the ribs. He said, "Oh!" like he'd been punched and sank to his knees. He touched the place the bullet went in and pulled away his hand, and it was like a red wet glove. Then he looked at me.

I felt goddamn bad about it just then. I thought I'd feel different, but I felt goddamn bad, like I felt when I shot Bell on the stairwell.

"You shot the hell out of me, Kid, I pissed in my pants."

I didn't know what to say.

"I got me a bottle under that wagon seat, could you reach it for me?"

I reached in under the seat and took out a bottle that was half full and pulled the cork and handed it to him. He took a drink, there on his knees, one hand holding on to the front wheel of the wagon for support. Some of the liquor spilled from his lips and down the front of his shirt and soaked in with the blood that was flowering across his middle.

He winced and said, "I wish to Christ you'd done a better job of it — this hurts like a son of a bitch, Kid."

"You didn't give me time to aim," I said.

"You would have killed me anyway — whether I reached for my gun or not. I did what I had to do."

I thought that he was probably right, but now, looking back on it, I can't say if I would have or not.

"It went in through my lungs. I'm as dead as anything."

"I guess that's how Charlie must have felt, and Tom," I said.

"Oh, Jesus, Bill, what have you done to me?"

He sat down on his haunches, placed his back against the wagon's wheel, splayed his legs out, his palsied hands shaking over the blood spot, looking down, looking back up at me.

"I guess I'm sorry I had to shoot you, Pat."

He twisted his mouth, said, "You ain't the only one."

"I'd go for help but you'd be dead before I got back."

"I got children, Kid, I tell you that?"

"Yes," I said and helped him take another drink of liquor.

"This whole fucking thing was wrong from the

get-go, wasn't it?" Some of the words sputtered from his lips, some blood dribbled out with the liquor.

"I feel a darkness in me."

"Does it hurt much, Pat?"

He shook his head.

"Not as bad as you'd think. Feel like I'm filling up with a cold darkness."

"You didn't give me no choice."

"Who you shitting, Kid? It was you who didn't give me no choice."

"Drink your liquor, Pat. No point in arguing about it now."

He took a big sigh and closed his eyes and I thought that done it, but then in a few minutes he opened his eyes again and said, "Charlie's waiting to take me over."

I don't know, it made the hair on the back of my neck stand up and I said to him that it was just the liquor but he shook his head and said, "No, Kid, Charlie is waiting, can't you see him?"

And I said, well, he'd best go on then and go with him, and Pat nodded and said, "See you on the other side, Kid."

That's how I remembered it and that's how I put it in my book and I know that Manuella was right — that killing Pat was a mean trick on my part and that I'd take his death and the other mean things I'd done to the grave with me.

They say Brazil killed him, or maybe Killin' Jim Miller or a drunken sheep-herder, the newspaper reported.

Brazil was acquitted in a court of law. Miller never charged. No sheep-herder found.

What's that tell you?

More bones buried in the loam
The night wind sings:
"I'm coming home,
I'm coming home."
Pistols and silver buckles.
Brass bullets and Mexican spurs.
Saddles and piebald mares.
Tumbleweeds & dry water holes.
Liquor & red shirts.
Blood & water.

How much longer will I see her sitting at the kitchen table staring at her glass birds, sipping her coffee, her head full of Charlie? All the women I loved, all the ones I had, I ended up with her. There had to be a reason. I just can't figure out quite what it was.

None that lived, I thought when Pat asked, did I have children.

51

**NO MATTER HOW I COUNT THE DAYS, THEY
ALWAYS TOTE UP TO ZERO.
— FROM THE JOURNAL OF HENRY MCCARTY**

Here is a list of the dead:

Clay Allison — lived forty-seven years. Fell under
a wagon drunk, died of a broken neck.
Sam Bass — lived twenty-seven years. Killed by
Texas Rangers.
Charlie Bowdre — lived twenty-two years. Shot
and killed by assassin.
Pat Garrett — lived fifty-eight years. Shot and
killed by assassin.
John Wesley Hardin — lived forty-three years.
Shot and killed by assassin.
J. B. "Wild Bill" Hickok — lived thirty-nine
years. Shot and killed by assassin.
John "Doc" Holliday — lived thirty-six years.
Died of consumption.
Tom Horn — lived forty-three years. Hanged.
Jesse James — lived thirty-five years. Shot and
killed by assassin.

Tom O'Folliard — lived twenty-six years. Shot and killed by assassin.

Henry Plummer — lived twenty-seven years. Hanged.

Johnny Ringo — lived thirty-eight years. Suicide.

John Henry Selman (killed Hardin) — lived fifty-seven years. Shot and killed by assassin.

Luke Short — lived thirty-nine years. Died of gunshot wounds.

Belle Starr — lived forty-one years. Shot and killed by assassin.

These I have listed in my book, names I am familiar with, some I knew, some I didn't. They are of little importance to me now — just names scratched upon the page in lines of blue and black ink on days when I could think of nothing better to write about, on days when the skies were dirty gray and rain dripped from the eaves and old wounds flared and gnawed at me like the sharp teeth of time. Days of boredom, random thoughts. Dead men, ghosts, writ in stone.

Like tin cans on a fence plunked by a .22 — *ping, ping, ping!*

They say Buffalo Bill got cancer of the ass and died from that. He met the queen of England, then got cancer of the ass. Imagine his regret.

They found Wyatt Earp behind the wheel of his flivver in the driveway of his home in Los Angeles. They say he loved that goddamn automobile more than sunlight and pussy. Dead of a heart attack, an old, old man.

Bat Masterson slumped at his desk in New York at the newspaper office where he worked, his heart, like Wyatt's, having failed him. He'd just finished refereeing a boxing match.

From a shelf above my bed I take a book of poetry by Lord Byron and read these words:

"And if I laugh at any mortal thing.
Tis that I may not weep."
And these: "Whom the gods love die young, was said of yore."

Byron, he was right.

Manuella is in love with her new Victrola and plays it constantly. The music is scratchy and sounds like the singers are standing in a well or a cave or something. She cranks the handle and carefully places the needle down on the record, then dances around the room until her heart starts to thump too fast and forces her to sit down at the kitchen table, where she listens, her eyes looking off somewhere beyond the sill of birds.

I find myself wanting to go for a long walk never to return. To walk and walk and just keep walking until I've used up the last of me and my own heart stops. I have the need to stand by a river, the Pecos or Rio Grande, and take in the murky scent of the water, to dip my hands in and wash my face and neck with the muddy cold drops and taste the silt of time.

I must have said something, cursed maybe, said, goddamn, for Manuella scolded me, saying, "Hush your profanity, Henry." Saying, "Listen, that's Al Jolsen singing." I didn't know what she was talking about.

My room and my books and my writing journal are all that I have left. A little more time maybe to get it all out, the thoughts I have in me still. My legs and feet are pale and ridged with tiny blue worms and are always cold and I remember what Pat said the afternoon I shot him:

"I feel like I'm filling up with darkness."

I wonder, when the time comes, will I add my name to the list of the dead, or will someone do that for me. I am surely not one that the gods loved, but one who danced with the devil in a holy cave where the angels dared not enter.

I feel myself filling with darkness.
Filling with darkness.

52

**DREAMS ARE JUST THE DEAD VISITING US.
— FROM THE JOURNAL OF HENRY MCCARTY**

In my moment of dreams (I'm not sure if they are really dreams) I am with Charlie and his skin is black as pitch, his eyes sightless, and we dance to music that rises up off the desert floor, and the voices of angels sprinkle our heads like summer rain.

"I hate you," he says, but laughingly so, "for your indiscretions with Billy." *Laugh, laugh, laugh.* "If I had known, I would have never brought him to the house that day to let him get a look at you." Charlie is swift and spins me, spins me until we are like dust devils whirling over a tan valley and turning into a single hot wind of dust spinning madly.

"You are a bittersweet thought to me, Manuella, knowing that you give yourself to him, that you spread your legs for him on moon-filled nights and thrust your hips into him feverishly. To know that he was inside you in that sacred place makes my heart bitter. But to know that you were not lonely and alone all this time . . ." His voice is a high wind swept away.

"Oh, Charlie, you are such a sad sweet fool for love," I say. *Laugh, laugh, laugh.* But tears sting my cheeks. "I only left with him because of Garrett. He vowed to kill us every one, put his pistols to our hearts and kill love and memory and kill our already dead hearts. That's why I left with Billy."

"Well, this I don't believe," Charlie says. *Laugh, laugh, laugh.* His hat pushed back to show his widow's peak of blue-black hair. "I think it was written in the stars that I would die at a young age, like in a tragic lover's ballad, so that you could go away with a new lover but leave your heart behind with me." *Whirling, whirling.*

"He's a peckerwood, that Bill is, for his deceit and treachery so that he could have you. He will be as faithless to you as he was to me and Tom. Tom loved him more than most women love their men. He made Tom laugh, but Tom don't laugh no more." *Laugh, laugh, laugh.*

"Dance with me, Charlie, to the tune of the white wind."

"Yes, yes, yes," he says. Faster and faster until the world spins out from beneath our feet and the stars shine in our eyes.

I am awakened by a pistol shot. Henry has just gone out to the porch, the pistol shot was the screen door slapping the jamb.

Henry sits muttering to himself. Hands moving as he talks, like as though he is talking to someone there on the porch with him, gesturing, pointing this way and that. But all that's there are cream-colored light and Henry.

"I'll tell you, goddamn it, there ain't no safe place to hide, so why run? Yes, sir, yes, sir, that's what I'm saying. Sure, I hear what you're saying, but do you hear what I'm saying? Uh-huh, yep. That's it, goddamn it, ain't that it? Uh-huh. *Yo tuve en caballo rapido una vez.* Joe! Joe! *Yo entrano bailando con la whores en le plaza.*"

He mutters and moves his hands, speaking in Spanish of fast horses and whores. I think maybe he is talking to Charlie. I think Charlie went from my dream to Henry's and they are talking about the old days together. I wonder if he is looking into Charlie's lifeless eyes, looking straight into his soul. Henry should taste the death bitter and burning on his tongue to know what it is like, to know what he has wrought upon others who loved him and died for him.

"Oh shit," he says, and his head drops like a weight and I think for one moment, my heart frozen in midbeat, that he is dead, that Charlie has come and taken him, has squeezed off the flow of his breath. His hands hang limply at his sides, the fingers nearly touching the floor — a lick of wind ruffles his hair.

Instead of going out and placing my ear to his chest, I turn and go into the room where he keeps his books and sit on the bed wanting and

318

waiting to understand what it was that caused him one day, years ago, to leave our bed and never return. Was it the power of words that seduced him? The ink and paper that replaced the flesh? The books lined upon the shelf neatly, their roaring silence bound gracefully by leathery skin. Speak to me, I pray, tell me what secrets you shared with my lover, this man now dead upon my porch in a high-back rocker.

From his hiding place I take the key and unlock the desk, looking for my redemption, for he has left me nothing but the words he so carefully scratched on the pages of his journal. I will read them, then burn them. I will watch the pages curl over in the flames and blacken into ash and feel the heat against my face.

I have the book in my hands when he coughs and the sound is like a cold finger on the back of my neck. I quickly put the book away and replace the key to its hiding place, then go and check on him.

"Jesus, you know," he says, "sometimes when I doze off like that it's like I'm falling down a dark, dark well and I'm never coming back. I think maybe one of these times I won't. Do you have any of that bark tea left?"

The bones in my hips ache and I wonder if it is my punishment for sins of the flesh. I quickly think of Mr. Miller — a handsome man with a horseless carriage — and the dry way he made love to me, the attentive eyes and scent of bay rum.

"Yes," I tell Henry, "I will get you a glass of bark tea."

"Do you think we go on, beyond the grave, I mean?" he says, droplets of tea on his lips, his gaze unfixed.

"Yes, to everlasting life for those who believe."

"And those who don't."

"Hell and damnation."

"Fire and brimstone, burning in a lake of fire, ain't that what your Bible says?"

"Yes."

"Do you think we will be separated in death, you and me, Manuella, or reunited? Or will it be you and Charlie who are reunited?"

"I've tried to live a good life." (The face of Miller is before me now, the sable eyes, the thin moustache, the hard small teeth.) "I don't know what happens except that the spirit lives on — the dead who aren't in heaven and aren't in hell are here among us — restless and yearning."

Miller's groping tongue is idiotic as it tries to worm its way into my mouth.

"You think Charlie is here with us?"

"Yes, I think so."

Miller's fingers pinch and probe, bruising my flesh.

"Tom too?"

Miller whispering his dry words in my ear, saying how he lusts for me.

"I don't know."

Miller saying, *Let me touch you, Manuella.*

"Garrett?"

Holy Mary, mother of God, pray for us sinners now and at the hour of our death.

"I think Pat Garrett is in hell where you sent him, Henry."

Miller forcing himself between my legs, the scraping of his moustache against my cheek.

Henry licks his lips, his tongue thick and fat.

Blessed is the fruit of thy womb.

"So I die, I go to hell, you die, you go to heaven, maybe someplace else, rid of me at last, eh. Maybe you and Charlie return to each other. Think he knows I come and took you, screwed you on the balcony in Niagara Falls for all the world to see? Took his woman?"

"It is an insult this way you talk to me after all these years, after the things you've done and I've put up with. Why do you still try to wound me with your words, Henry? Why?"

A look of sadness crosses his face, dims his eyes.

"I guess because I know I can," he says. "I guess I learned how easy it was and couldn't stop myself from using what I learned on you. You were always weak to me in that way, Manuella. You were with Charlie and you were with me and your weakness showed. You don't think I know about Miller, but I know. You let us use you and we did because we could. You've always had the vulnerability of a wounded bird."

Miller withdrawing from me, his eyes glazed.

I cover my face with my hands because I don't want to look at Henry or have him look at me.

"I hate you for your words," I say.

"I know."

A black automobile rushes down the street.

His hands take my face and hold it and he says:

"In spite of everything, I still care about you. It has never been my intention to hurt you, I don't know why I do." Then his hands drop away and he goes to his room and locks the door behind him.

I remember an ancient song of the native people:

A bird will come and take you
Its wings spread across the sky
To the heavens it will carry you
Do not cry, do not cry.

My mother sang these words to me when I was small and frightened of the thunder or when I fell and scraped my knee, and once when I was stung by a scorpion and got its fever in my blood. She would rock me in her arms and sing this song to me and soon my tears would stop and I would feel peaceful and safe against her, her arms holding me tightly, shutting out the world of fearful things, her breath sweetly warm upon my face.

Do not cry, do not cry.

Miller saying how grateful he was, putting money on the table next to the bed.

And heaven seems so far away.

53

**WE ARE BORN ALONE AND WE DIE ALONE.
THE EARTH IS RICH WITH OUR BONES AND
WOMEN WEEP WITH THE PAIN OF NEW LIFE.
MORE BONES FOR THE HEAP.
— FROM THE JOURNAL OF HENRY McCARTY**

I can't stop my hands from shaking, for death is near, I can feel it. Like I'm filling up with darkness, isn't that what Garrett said the day I killed him? I hear her weeping in the other room. Her Jesus should know this: I never meant to hurt her. I despised her at times for not being what I wanted, for not being Susan McSween or Celsa Gutierrez or Isabella. I despised her at all times for not being the prostitute Mariel in Cuba. I despised her for being Charlie's wife and for what she'd done with Mr. Miller, that rich man in New York who owned the shoe factory where she worked while I was gone off to war. And yet, it made me desire her too. I don't know, I don't know. My mind plays tricks on me so often these days. I thought I saw Charlie earlier, out there on the porch, and we were arguing about how to outfox Garrett, him wanting to go one way — up through the Capitan Pass — me saying how we should ride south to Mesilla. Charlie could argue like a son of a bitch at times, whereas Tom went along with anything I said.

Listen, did you hear that? Sounds like thunder. I always liked a good storm. Nights of lying abed with a woman in your arms, the rattle of rain off the window glass, the flashes of lightning — the shattering of thunder. I was born of water, a woman in Santa Fe told me once. She read palms and she read mine and said I was born of water and would live a long and fruitful life and turn out to be prosperous. She was right about the long life. I think I'm nearly ninety years old — can't remember exactly the day I was born, although Garrett's man, Ash Upson, put my date of birth as November 23, 1859. How true that is I couldn't say, but it seems to me Mother said I was born when the dandelions were in bloom. Can't say, can't say. My mind won't sit still for more than a minute.

Manuella says I should go and see a priest and make a final confession before it's too late. She says I should try and save my soul. I said, save it from what? I know such things hurt her, just like me saying what I said earlier. I don't know why I have this need to hurt her when I've spent most of my life trying to protect her. I think she knows that down deep, or why else would she have stayed with me all these years? Why else would she have given up the opportunity to maybe marry a rich man like Miller who — I could see in his eyes the day I talked to him — would have given her anything she wanted? Why else would she have stayed with me if she didn't know that deep down I did everything I could to keep her from harm? A woman knows what's in a man's heart even if he doesn't say it. She acts like she doesn't care, like she'd as soon see me dead. Maybe she would. But if that's true, why would she worry about my soul, tell me to go see a priest?

Love is shapeless.

I have a pocket Bible that Isabella gave to me. It is small and has a gold cross embossed on it and is written in Spanish. Though I can speak the lingo, I never learned to read it. Sometimes I open its pages and pretend to know what it says. But I don't know, it could be saying anything. All I know about this magnificent God it speaks of is what Manuella and other women have told me over the years. I wonder why, if God is as good as they say he is, he allows so much innocent blood to be shed? Why would he let those boys shoot Tunstall in the face, or let McSween be murdered? Men killed simply because they believe in something and cannot stand injustice. But more than that, why would God pass the sins of the father on to the son? My children all dead — his too. I would never stand still and watch my boy being murdered. So it makes me wonder about this God of Manuella's, this God of women, and why I should go and confess my sins to another man. She goes to the church every morning dressed in a black dress, carrying her beads, and comes back an hour later and sits and stares at her birds. What does she get from this confession of her soul?

She says, *pray*. I don't know how.

She bows her head and closes her eyes and moves her lips soundlessly, talking to God or Charlie or somebody, smoke curling up from her cigarette, her coffee growing cold in a blue cup.

Of all the things I will miss, this life I've led is not one of them.

I am filling up with darkness.
I am not afraid.
Charlie and Tom wait for me
There in the garden by the
Pecos, by the singing river
Of our regret and sorrow.

I am not afraid.

54

I GUESS I ALWAYS KNEW SOMEDAY IT WOULD HAPPEN. DEATH WOULD COME A-KNOCKING AND I WOULDN'T BE WEARING MY GUNS.
— FROM THE JOURNAL OF HENRY McCARTY

He calls me to his room. I am surprised. His voice is weak, a croak of sound, utterances, and asks would I sit by the bed. He has dressed himself neatly in a dark suit, black coat, white shirt with pearl buttons, black trousers, socks and shoes.

"How do I look?" he says.

"Like you are going someplace fancy, on a trip."

"I am," he says.

"Where to?"

He smiles with his eyes.

"You know where."

"Then it is time?"

"Yes. I'm filling up with darkness. It will be soon now."

"Are you afraid?" I ask.

He shakes his head.

"No. Well, maybe some."

I take his hand in mine, feel the waxy fingers, the warm flesh as delicate as rice paper. The hand is covered with brown, irregular spots like old maps. They are small hands.

"Would you like me to read to you?"

He closes his eyes for a brief moment, then opens them again. They are a milky blue, a mixture of cloud and sky.

"Do you have pain?" I ask.

"Just here," he says, tapping his chest above his heart and smiles again.

"Why there?"

"The pain I gave to you has come back to me now."

"It's okay," I say.

I feel his fingers feebly squeeze my own.

"We were like a dream," he says, "a long and endless dream."

"Not all of it bad, Henry."

He swallows, the bob of his throat sliding under the loose skin of his neck. He hasn't shaved in several days and I think that the least I should do is go and get his razor and shave him and comb his hair.

His gaze shifts from me to somewhere in the room, then back to me.

"Thought I heard . . ."

"What?"

"I'm not sure."

I touch his face, feel that the warmth has left him.

"Read something to me," he says.

I reach for his journal and he shakes his head.

"No, not that."

"They are your words, Henry, your history. Don't you want to hear them one last time?"

"No, no. I left them for you. Maybe you could sell it, let people know the truth: that Garrett never shot me that night — there's people who would pay good money for the memoirs of Billy the Kid. You could use the money . . ."

"Do you think anyone would believe it?"

He beckons me close, his words now a rasp, for he is down to the last ones God has allotted him.

"If Jesus died and lived again . . . why not me?"

I kiss his lips and he closes his eyes.

I take from the shelf a book by Shakespeare and read these words from a place he'd marked with a red ribbon:

> The web of our life is of a mingled yarn, good and ill together: our virtues would be proud if our faults whipped them not, and our crimes would despair if they were not cherished by our virtues.

And underlined later on the page is this:

Praising what is lost
Makes the remembrance dear.

He sighs and opens his eyes and looks at me

with a look of deep content, as though he has tasted the apple of the garden and it is sweet to him even though the fruit is forbidden, and he is not ashamed of his nakedness as I have been, but rather pleased and proud of the way he has gone through life. A man with nothing to hide from the world except himself. I think he never told others who he was, never came forth, in order to protect me somehow.

His eyes brighten for a moment and he says:

"Did I ever dance with you in Mesilla?"

"No, you never did."

"I should have."

"Yes, you should have."

Then, with a voice barely audible, he whispers:

"I love you."

55

He is buried in a simple, unmarked grave near a river, as he requested.

"Let the water come and take me, for I was born of water. Let it wash my bones to the sea, and put no cross upon my grave, for I don't want the mark of another murdered man to watch over me."

And there you will find him, in the Garden of Stone — only his grave bears no flower.

Time is a steady ticking in my wrist
& sometimes Charlie comes to visit,
but never Billy, and when I ask Charlie
about him, he says:
"I saw him last, riding toward old Fort Sumner,
Him and Garrett on white horses."

EPILOGUE

On or about midnight on July 14, 1881, it is said that Patrick Floyd Garrett entered the home of Pedro Maxwell in the village of Fort Sumner, New Mexico, and that while there, sitting on the side of the half-awake Maxwell's bed, questioning him, Billy Bonney, known as Kid, or "the Kid," entered the residence. Garrett, claiming to recognize the Kid even though it was pitch dark, drew his revolver and fired twice at the shadowy figure, then ran from the house, shouting he had killed the Kid. Even by his own testimony, Garrett admits to being questioned about the validity of the identity of the man he shot by his own deputies, Poe and McKinney. The shooting was followed by a hastily assembled coroner's jury — one man of which was Garrett's relative by marriage — and it was ascertained that the dead youth was indeed Billy the Kid. An equally hasty burial was arranged in the old fort cemetery (some claim that the Kid's body was simply wrapped in a horse blanket), and that was the end of a legend. Historians have debated whether it was really the Kid whom Garrett killed that night with what was a truly lucky shot, or if it was someone else. For years those who claimed to have known him said that the Kid was still alive. In fact, the novelist Walter Nobel Burns, in preparation for writing his book *The Saga of Billy the Kid*, interviewed many people throughout New Mexico who claimed they knew the Kid and that he had not been killed that night. Even as late as the 1950s a man named "Brushy" Bill Roberts claimed to be the Kid, offering ample evidence that he well could have been the notorious outlaw.

There is no physical evidence that the grave in the old fort cemetery contains anything, not even bones, since it has always been quite common for the Pecos River that runs through the area to flood its banks frequently. Floods, in fact, swept away the Maxwell house where the shooting took place, and floods have often carried away the caskets and remains of the dead. Even Garrett states this in his book, *The Authentic Life of Billy the Kid*, written a year after the shooting. It would be nearly impossible to prove one way or the other that the Kid was killed that night, or if he made yet another fantastic escape from his pursuers. Copies of his extant letters prove that the Kid was neither a simple, uneducated boy nor a homicidal maniac. Billy had escaped death's sentence more than once, and as recently as just a few months before the shooting.

Did the Kid live, change his name, and remove himself from the territory? It is conceivable. And what are we to make of Garrett's own murder almost thirty years later in the White Sands region? No one was ever found guilty and there are many theories as to who might have committed the crime, including the Kid himself.

The Stone Garden is merely one writer's vision of a ghost that has been haunting him for nearly fifty years.